Shay swiped a damp paper to___ ___er Vicki's face.

"There, beautifu___ ___
Daddy?"

Shay angled her ___ ___ ___ding
Vicki toward him___ ___

Mark's throat closed, emotion making it impossible to breathe. The sight of his daughter balanced on Shay's hip and snuggled against her was wrenchingly poignant. It should have been comical, those sparkly red hearts sticking out of Vicki's mass of curls and Shay standing there with a too-small tiara perched on her head.

I could love this woman.

Dear Reader,

When my son was much younger, he was in speech therapy and I remember being anxious for the day when he could share whatever he was thinking without any communication obstacles. Well, I got my wish. He has shared *many* things with a great many people.

In this book, single father Mark Hathaway is about to learn that you can't always predict what kids will say…and that sometimes they share information you wish they hadn't. More than anything, Mark's six-year-old daughter wants a mother and, when it becomes clear that her father is too busy with his job to date, she takes matters into her own small hands, landing Mark in the principal's office.

New principal Shay Morgan stepped into the role midyear when the former, much beloved, principal retired early for medical reasons. Shay is hoping to make a good impression so she will be hired permanently. Flirting with one of the students' fathers would be a bad career move, especially a father whose first few attempts at classroom volunteering don't go well. But Shay can't help admiring how hard Mark works on his daughter's behalf and how he keeps trying. She also can't help noticing that he has a great smile and an adorable kid.

As Mark and Shay discover, even when we've meticulously mapped out our priorities, life and love (and our children!) often surprise us.

Happy Valentine's,

Tanya Michaels

His Valentine Surprise

TANYA MICHAELS

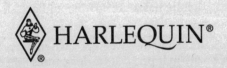

HARLEQUIN®

TORONTO • NEW YORK • LONDON
AMSTERDAM • PARIS • SYDNEY • HAMBURG
STOCKHOLM • ATHENS • TOKYO • MILAN • MADRID
PRAGUE • WARSAW • BUDAPEST • AUCKLAND

Recycling programs
for this product may
not exist in your area.

ISBN-13: 978-0-373-75347-5

HIS VALENTINE SURPRISE

Copyright © 2011 by Tanya Michna

This edition published by arrangement with Harlequin Books S.A.

For questions and comments about the quality of this book
please contact us at Customer_eCare@Harlequin.ca

www.eHarlequin.com

Printed in U.S.A.

ABOUT THE AUTHOR

Tanya Michaels began telling stories almost as soon as she could talk...and started stealing her mom's Harlequin romances less than a decade later. In 2003, Tanya was thrilled to have her first book, a romantic comedy, published by Harlequin Books. Since then, Tanya has sold more than twenty books and is a two-time recipient of a Booksellers' Best Award as well as a finalist for the Holt Medallion, National Readers' Choice Award and Romance Writers of America's prestigious RITA® Award. Tanya lives in Georgia with her husband, two children and an unpredictable cat, but you can visit Tanya online at www.tanyamichaels.com.

Books by Tanya Michaels

If you ever have to meet a summer writing deadline while the kids are out of school and underfoot, I highly suggest that in addition to a wonderful husband and mother (both of which I am blessed to have) you arm yourself with a team of incomparable friends. Thank you to Ashley Cate, Sally Kilpatrick, Melissa Silva and their families— my very own superhero squad.

Prologue

I hate you, Santa Claus!

Six-year-old Vicki Hathaway sat at her aunt's dining room table, remembering how Aunt Dee took her to that mall in Charlotte to go Christmas shopping. Vicki had her picture made with Santa and told him what she wanted, *really* wanted, more than anything in the world. And because her dad said it was bad to be greedy, she'd only asked for one thing.

A new mommy.

But December was over and now it was almost the end of January. Her father hadn't met any new women or gone on one single date. How could Santa not help her when she'd been *so* good? Her babysitter, Mrs. Norris, called her an angel. Vicki had been almost perfect, except for spilling juice on her dad's inventory papers—which didn't count because it was an accident—and sometimes fighting with her cousin Bobby (which didn't count since he always started it by picking on her).

"Vicki," her aunt said, "is everything all right? You're not eating. And you love pot roast. I made it especially for you."

Vicki loved almost all the food at Aunt Dee's house. Her dad was not a good cook, which was why they ate most nights at the Braeden Burger Shop. Except on Tuesdays when Aunt Dee picked Vicki up from ballet and Vicki's dad came here after he closed the store and they had dinner together. Tonight, Vicki wasn't hungry. Her tummy had hurt since ballet class, but she didn't want to tell Aunt Dee. Her aunt would make her drink that pink stuff that tasted *dee*-sgusting.

Vicki's stomach had started to feel bad when her dance teacher reminded everyone about the big April recital and said she was sending home notes to ask for volunteer "stage moms." Lorelai Moon said right away that her mother could come.

Lorelai's mom was in charge of the children's choir at church and came to their elementary school to read to the first graders after math centers. Lorelai's mom was in the PTA with Aunt Dee. Lorelai's mom also baked the cupcakes for their ballet class Christmas party. Vicki was the only girl in ballet—the only girl in the whole first grade—who didn't have a mother.

Her eyes hurt, and her throat felt sore like the time she got so sick she could hardly swallow. "I'm not hungry."

Vicki's dad looked up from his plate. He hadn't said much tonight, and Vicki thought he looked sad. He looked like that a lot lately, probably because he was lonely.

"You didn't work up an appetite in dance class, Vicki-bug?" he asked.

She shrugged. "Can I be excused?"

Aunt Dee frowned at her, and Vicki thought she would say no. But sometimes grown-ups surprised you. "I guess you can go up to Bobby's room while we finish our meal. Bobby, you got some new board games for

Christmas. I'm sure your cousin would enjoy playing with you."

Not really. The main thing in the house Vicki liked playing with was Butterscotch, her aunt's poodle. But they always put the dog outside during meals.

"I'm eleven!" Bobby whined. For a big kid, he whined a lot. "The games I got aren't for six-year-olds. Besides, I have homework. You said I could use your computer to do my report."

Aunt Dee's computer was in her office, with a door that shut. "Can we both go in your office?" Vicki asked. "Bobby can do his report, and I'll bring Butterscotch in there with us. Then she couldn't beg."

After Aunt Dee agreed, Vicki followed her cousin into the office.

Bobby spoke to her in his usual mean tone. "This is important schoolwork, so don't bother me, okay?"

"I won't!" Why would she want to talk to Bobby? He was a jerk.

When she sat down, she patted her knees so Butterscotch would come to her. She put her arms around the dog and hugged the poodle, burying her face in the soft fur. Aunt Dee took Butterscotch to the groomer every week, so the dog smelled like fancy shampoo.

Vicki sniffed and sniffed again. She didn't know when she'd started crying. But now she couldn't stop.

"Hey!" Bobby sounded scared. "Stop that. They're gonna think I did something to you. Knock it off."

"I—I can't."

"What are you even crying for?"

"B-because I don't have a m-mom."

He shut up. Even Bobby wasn't a big enough jerk to tease her about that. Instead, he sat down on the floor on the other side of Butterscotch to pet her, his fingers bumping against Vicki's arm.

"Do you remember her?" he asked. "You were just a little kid when she died."

That was funny because he called her a little kid now. She couldn't answer him, though, because she was crying too hard.

"Aunt Jessica was pretty great," Bobby said. "I told her once I wanted to be a scientist and thought she might laugh at me, but she gave me a microscope for my birthday."

Vicki's dad bought her birthday presents, but he didn't wrap them. He just stuck them in a bag. Sometimes Aunt Dee used bags, too, but when she did, there were bows on the outside and colored paper tucked in with the gift.

"I need a mother." She rubbed the snot off her nose. "Santa Claus was supposed to bring me one, but he didn't." Spring would be here in a few months—Vicki learned all about seasons back in kindergarten—so maybe she could ask the Easter Bunny for help.

Bobby opened his mouth and took a breath. He looked like he was about to start explaining stuff, like when he'd bored her that one time talking about different kinds of rocks. Then he shook his head. "You don't need Santa, kid, you need Promises Dot Com."

"Promises?" Vicki knew about "dot com." Sometimes her dad let her use his computer to play games; plus her teacher, Mrs. Frost, sent them to different websites to practice phonics or math facts. But she hadn't been able to work on her dad's laptop much lately. He was too busy with stuff for the store to share.

"Haven't you ever seen one of those sappy Promises

commercials?" Bobby asked. "People meet each other on the computer, through email and messages, and start dating. Your dad would have to sign up."

Vicki wasn't sure he would do that. "If he meeted her on the computer, how would I know if I liked her?"

"*Met,* doofus. Maybe he's already met someone," Bobby said. "I mean, not on the computer, but in real life. He could date someone from church or our school. That way, you'd know immediately if you liked her."

"But he doesn't talk to any of those ladies from church or school."

Bobby's forehead got all squiggly, the way it did when he was thinking really hard. "Do you know what a Sadie Hawkins Dance is?"

"No."

"They had one at the middle school. The girls ask the guys to be their dates. Maybe we can get a woman to ask out Uncle Mark."

"How?" And who? Vicki's Sunday school teacher, ballet teacher and first-grade teacher were all married.

Bobby stood up, looking at all of the stuff on his mom's desk. He picked up a little yellow book that had the words *Woodside PTA* on the front. "If I helped you find a mom, you guys probably wouldn't be over here so much."

"You'll help? Really?"

Nodding, he flipped open the book. "I have a plan."

Vicki had stopped crying already. Now she smiled and hugged Bobby. "Thank you, thank you, thank you!"

It was a weird day when you could trust your jerky cousin more than you could trust Santa Claus.

Chapter One

"Wakey-wakey, eggs and bakey." The ridiculous rhyme rolled off Mark Hathaway's tongue from habit—it had been the way Jess used to cajole their daughter out of bed for preschool.

Although Vicki had more practice getting up early and getting ready for school, she was no more cheerful about it now than she had been at three. Muttering something that was no doubt a variation of "go away," his first grader scooted farther beneath the pony-print comforter. Not even the curly top of her head was visible.

With a sigh, he flipped back the corner of her blanket. "Up and at 'em, Vicki-bug. You have school, and Daddy has an important meeting this morning. Tomorrow's Saturday, we'll both sleep late then, okay?" If today's breakfast meeting went well maybe he'd finally be able to get a decent night's sleep.

"Don't feel good," she muttered. It was her standard second line of defense, after hiding beneath the covers.

"What hurts?" When she didn't answer, he placed a hand over her forehead. "You don't have a fever. Come on, hurry up so you can help me pick out your clothes.

How about…your orange bathing suit with some polka-dot socks?"

Some mornings, his attempts at humor were only met with a sleepy glare. Today, he was rewarded with a half giggle.

"I can't wear a bathing suit to school, Daddy! And plus it's winter." She sighed, clutching her stuffed horse close. "Do I have to get out of bed?"

"'Fraid so."

"Hug first?" she pleaded. Of all her regular procrastination techniques, this was his favorite.

"Absolutely." He sat at the foot of her bed, leaning back along the wall, and she scooted into his lap, snuggling against him. He kissed her on top of the head, breathing in the apple-scented detangler he'd combed through her unruly hair last night. Even with the spray-conditioner, she still winced when he hit a knot. And he was completely hopeless when it came to fixing her hair for ballet class—he barely managed simple pony-tails and barrettes for school. The coppery curls were untamable. No matter what style he attempted, it ended up lopsided.

With his everyday shortcomings, it was little wonder the poor kid had been dropping hints for the past few months. Mark was not oblivious to the fact that his daughter yearned for a mother figure. Thank God for Dee, Jessica's older sister. How would he have survived the past two years without his sister-in-law's help?

If the store closed, would Vicki have to move away from her aunt and uncle? The knot of dread which had recently taken up residence in his chest tightened. *She's already lost too much.* No little girl should have to grow up without a mother. How could he possibly take her away from her friends and family in Braeden, North Carolina, the only home she'd ever known?

He tried to shake off the omnipresent worry. Extra stress wouldn't change the outcome of today's meeting. Besides, he'd been working quite a few extra hours lately, and Vicki deserved the benefit of his full attention.

"You know I love you, right, Bug?"

"Love you, too."

"We make a good team, you and me."

"Teams can be *lots* of people," she said. "Like when Coach B splits us up to play kickball at school. Two isn't very many."

Her words sliced through him, her delicate suggestion that, much as he loved her, he wasn't enough.

Mark chose his response carefully. "Two might not sound like very many, but when you think about it, we have plenty of other people who love us. Aunt Dee, Uncle Frank and Bobby, Mrs. Norris, Lucy at the store, Cade…"

Cade Montgomery had become Mark's best friend since Jess died—because the sometime white-water-rafting guide, sometime carpenter was single. It was so much less awkward to hang out with Cade than all the married couples Mark and Jessica had known. Cade was about as confirmed a bachelor as a man could get, but he was surprisingly good with Vicki. He'd even promised to come to her ballet recital.

Of course, he'd later asked Mark if any of the little ballerinas had hot single moms.

Mark sighed. "Honey, is this about wanting a mom?"

"Will I ever have one?"

He knew the answer she wanted to hear, but the few

dates he'd had in the past two years had left him cold. And even if he had more interest in the idea, he would put it on the back burner right now while he tried to sort out his job situation. Providing a stable home and financial security for his daughter were his priority.

"Someday, maybe." It was the best he could offer her without being dishonest.

"Are you shy?" she asked. "We talked about shy at school, like when you don't know how to make a new friend or are nervous to sing in music class. If you feel shy with girls, I can help!"

He grinned at that, imagining his six-year-old coaching him through first-date nerves. "You can, huh? Well, that's very nice of you, but it will have to wait until later. Right now, you need to get ready for school. We're already running late."

"Okay." She sat up, patting him on the shoulder. "But don't worry, Daddy. I have a plan. A good one."

Oh, boy. Part of him was amused and curious, wanting to ask his inventive daughter for details. On the other hand, he'd rather not encourage her Mommy Quest. It had wrecked him when he opened the letter to Santa she'd given Mark to mail—the one she'd insisted on writing all by herself. Mark had tried throughout November and December to get her to tell him what she wanted for Christmas, but she'd coyly refused to answer. Anxious to make sure "Santa" met her request, he'd finally seen it spelled out in green crayon. As a result, he'd overcompensated in the toys he'd bought her. She'd seemed delighted with them on Christmas morning, but after a week had passed, she'd turned pensive again.

Maybe if they didn't discuss her "plan" to overcome his supposed shyness with the ladies, she'd eventually forget about it. Yet even as he wanted to cling to that hope, he knew better. Vicki had inherited her mother's curly locks and big brown eyes—but she had Mark's stubborn streak.

THE STORE MARK RAN WAS called Up A Creek, a tongue-in-cheek name for a place that sold sporting goods and equipment for outdoor recreation. Right now, however, *up a creek* seemed entirely apt for his situation. This breakfast felt too much like a last meal.

Across the table, Bennett Coleridge, owner of the dozen or so Up A Creek locations, looked sympathetic as he picked up the syrup pitcher. "Understand, if I do close the store, there are still opportunities in the company for you. We have other sites. The one in South Carolina is closest, although if you wanted a complete change, our two stores in Colorado stay busy all year round."

And busy meant profitable.

When Up A Creek had first opened in Braeden, North Carolina, there had been a campground just outside of town and a popular lodge half an hour beyond that which offered hiking and kayaking excursions. Both had unfortunately closed in the past couple of years. Now it seemed as if the store Mark managed might be next to succumb to tough economic times.

Bennett had mentioned the possibility of Colorado if the Hathaways "wanted a complete change." But Vicki had been born here, had spent her entire life in the same house. For her, anything outside Braeden limits would be an overwhelming change. Mark knew that his personal life—or lack thereof—disappointed his daughter. How could he tell her that he was a failure professionally, too?

That she'd have to move away from her school and her friends?

He swallowed hard, determined to sound calm. Businessmen like Bennett were swayed by numbers, not desperation. "I know the store's profits have dipped." Around here, some folks were working two jobs to make ends meet, sacrificing their free time for recreation; others had been laid off, without the funds to maintain a hobby.

"But I have some ideas that might help turn things around," Mark said. He sounded passably convincing.

Bennett raised an eyebrow. "Such as?"

"Well, a few months ago I spoke to Principal Ridenour about sponsoring a booth at the elementary school's spring Fitness Fair. It's an all-day event local coaches and doctors started last year to educate parents on the risks of childhood obesity. In addition to the information, they provide stations that demonstrate fun ways the kids can keep in shape. It's a perfect platform for us. I can do a small-scale climbing wall, remind parents about the importance of bike helmets and staying hydrated, give out promotional coupons for items that will pull them into the store.

"Speaking as a dad," he continued, "parents are more willing to spend on their kids during lean times than on themselves. Especially if it means keeping the kids healthier."

Belatedly, Mark recalled that Principal Ridenour had retired over the holidays. He should really get in touch with the man's replacement.

"I'm all for this fitness fair thing," Bennett said, "but increased sales in canteens and junior knee pads aren't—"

"Also, I recently read a business article," Mark said quickly, "about how people who used to travel to luxury resorts or other countries are looking for less expensive domestic vacations. Let's face it, not many of us can afford to go to Aspen or Vail. People who live right here or in neighboring states, however, might be able to indulge in a day at Sugar Mountain more easily than they realized. There are several ski resorts within a hundred-mile radius of Braeden, but the newest one, Hawk Summit, is only a forty-minute drive. Their projected grand opening last year got delayed twice due to construction and when they finally did open for the season, unusual weather conditions hurt their bottom line. They're in their second season now and I'd guess they're struggling."

Bennett set his fork down with a reproachful sigh. "So you think a fledgling ski resort that's in danger of going under itself is somehow going to save a store that's going under?"

Mark felt his jaw tightening and forced himself to relax. "I think we can help each other, yes. And because they are, as you say, 'fledgling,' they have a bigger incentive to participate in some of the cross-promotional discount ideas I have. Bennett, I know I can turn the store around. I just need time, and—"

"Until the end of April," the other man interrupted, his tone final. "My wife and I are coming to the area for her high school's twentieth reunion. You and I will look at the numbers that week to determine whether or not there's been significant improvement over last spring. If not…"

Mark wouldn't let the reprieve go to waste. For the next three months, he would bust his butt and try everything he could think of to make Up A Creek a success. He owed it to his employees, who needed their paychecks, and his boss, who was giving him this chance. But most of all, he owed it to his daughter.

SHAY MORGAN PULLED HER CAR into the slot marked Reserved For Principal. Just a few weeks ago, seeing those words had filled her with enthusiasm and pride. While she was still proud that she'd been appointed the interim principal to finish out the year, well…it had been a long week. But today was Friday, which meant she'd soon have forty-eight hours to recharge, minus the stress of a family dinner Sunday evening.

Maybe the roads will be too icy for me to make the drive.

What she wanted to do was hole up in the cozy warmth of her house with a good book, free from pointed looks from a staff and faculty who were testing her authority, free from "helpful advice" from well-meaning parents who had limited knowledge of the county policies Shay was required to follow and free from the quiet disapproval of the school secretary, Roberta Cree.

Roberta had been at Woodside Elementary since it first opened its doors in 1987 and had outlasted all four previous principals, including Shay's immediate predecessor, the Esteemed Jonathan Ridenour Who Could Do No Wrong. The corridor that led from the main reception area to Shay's private office was lined with gold-framed portraits of the prior principals. She swore their eyes followed her whenever she passed. And the principals of yesteryear probably shook their heads at her when no one was looking.

All in all, her first month at Woodside hadn't gone

as smoothly as expected. Even though years had passed since she'd first voiced her ambition to become a principal, she could too clearly hear her father's words in her head. *You don't need those administrative headaches, sweetie. Why not stay a teacher, with only your classroom to worry about and summers off to focus on your own kids?*

Not that Shay had any kids. Or a husband. Or even a steady boyfriend.

She was currently between relationships, which seemed to worry her parents. After climbing out of the car, she shut her door—resisting the juvenile urge to slam it. Her brother, Bastien the M.D., didn't have a girlfriend. He practically lived at the hospital, and both parents applauded his lofty career goals as building a solid foundation for the future. When Bastien had declared he wanted to go to medical school, their father had never once suggested he settle for being a school nurse and take the summers off! So why the heck couldn't Shay get the same support for *her* professional aspirations? After all, it was a lifetime of listening to her mother—a retired elementary school teacher—that had inspired Shay in the first place. Mrs. Morgan and her teaching colleagues had been full of great ideas but lacked the power to implement them. Shay had decided early that she wanted to work her way up the scholastic ladder so that she could one day help teachers.

But so far, it was slow going at Woodside—an elementary school too small to have an assistant principal who might have been an ally in easing the transition. Maybe some of the faculty felt that warming to Shay too quickly would be disloyal to Esteemed Principal Ridenour. Everyone had been shocked by his heart attack in

November and sorry to see him leave the school when he took early retirement midyear. Perhaps Shay's eagerness to tackle her new position after the winter break had come across as unseemly, as if she were seizing on someone else's misfortune.

I will win these people over, she promised herself. After all, she was pretty darn likable. She was also truly passionate about providing a wonderful environment and the best education possible for the students of the small elementary school. In theory, her advocacy for their well-being gave her common ground with everyone else who set foot inside the door.

Like, for instance, the PTA president.

Shay sighed when she saw that exact woman pacing outside the school's front office, talking in low, tense tones with two other mothers. Shay recognized one of them as Carolyn Moon. The mom of a first grader, a third grader and fourth-grade twins, Carolyn seemed to spend as much time on school property as Shay did. Shay couldn't remember off the top of her head who the third woman was, but she looked just as unhappy as her companions. Thankfully, the trio kept their voices diplomatically soft—the students making their way to class before the first bell rang seemed oblivious to whatever the problem was.

If Shay were shorter, she might have given in to the temptation to blend in with a few of the fifth graders and slip past the mothers lying in wait. The PTA president, Nancy, was a sweet woman who truly cared about the student body, but she was a very anxious "the sky is falling" sort. She seemed perpetually worried that the school teetered on the brink of disaster and that, as president, she would be at the helm of the ship when it sank. It didn't help to have a second-in-command like Carolyn Moon, who complained about everything, upsetting Nancy's already-nervous disposition. Shay had learned quickly that finding Carolyn waiting for her outside the office was never a good way to start the day.

I can handle this. I am the principal, and I got this job because I am good at what I do. Shay pasted a wide, welcoming smile on her face and vowed that while she certainly encouraged dialogue from concerned parents, she was not going to let herself be ambushed before she'd even had a chance to pour a cup of coffee.

"Good morning, ladies," she said as they descended on her, all talking at once.

"Ms. Morgan," Carolyn began, "do you have any idea—"

Nancy cleared her throat and gave a surreptitious shake of her head. "Principal Morgan, we're sure you have a very full day, but—"

"I would be happy to find a few minutes in the schedule to chat with you," Shay assured them, "but right now, I need to prepare for the morning announcements. If the three of you want to wait, I'll be back as soon as I can. If you have somewhere else you need to be, please email me with anything you need to discuss. Or see Roberta about setting up an appointment."

"This should be addressed immediately!" Carolyn insisted. "A person can't just spam—"

"We'll wait," Nancy said firmly, shooting another look at her fellow PTA board member. Carolyn, this year's vice president, was clearly champing at the bit for her chance to be commander in chief, figuratively speaking.

Although Carolyn seemed like the type who might not realize it was figurative.

Shay agreed to return as soon as she could, then allowed herself to get caught up in the swell of children sent to the front office with various "please excuse Diane's absence yesterday" and "please allow Johnny to ride home on the bus with his friend" notes that had to be filed. The thirty minutes between when the front doors first opened to students and when morning announcements began were always hectic for the administrative staff.

Today, the usual cacophony of voices was dominated by two boys, each claiming that a pair of mittens in the office Lost and Found belonged to him. One boy was wailing that his mother had sworn he'd never see his Nintendo DS again if he lost another article of winter clothing this year. Roberta was trying to arbitrate the dispute. The five-foot-tall secretary had hair exactly like steel wool and she owned a sweater set in every color invented.

"You boys are much too loud," Shay said in quiet counterpoint to their shouting. "It's disrespectful to Mrs. Cree and to everyone else in the office."

Roberta looked up, including Shay in the pursed-lip censure she'd bestowed on the arguing boys. "I can handle this if you'd prefer to go check your email."

No doubt whatever those mothers outside the office were flustered about would be explained by the contents of Shay's in-box. Bypassing the coffeemaker, Shay left the boys in Roberta's custody and made a beeline for her office. Once inside she shut her door and entered her password, braced for the worst.

Whatever she'd been expecting, it certainly hadn't

been a plea from a student, soliciting dates for her father. Apparently, an email had gone out to the hundred and fifty or so families on the PTA mailing list. At least eleven parents had forwarded Shay a copy. The letter appeared to have come from Dee Riggs, the chairperson in charge of both the school's autumn and spring book fairs. But the subject line of the email stated, *From Victoria Hathaway*. It seemed that Victoria was trying to boost her father's love life in hopes of eventually getting a new mother.

Did Dee Riggs even realize yet that her email account had been hijacked in this manner? Given the number of parents who had already contacted Shay, surely someone had emailed Dee or planned to call her. Shay would talk to the woman today. First, however, she needed to have a few words with Victoria Hathaway's father and sole guardian.

Shay leaned forward and pressed the intercom button on her phone. "Roberta? I need you to get me—"

"He's already on his way."

Chapter Two

Most days, Mark's employer was in Colorado, oblivious to Mark's daily schedule. So why, the one day when Bennett was in town and wanted to see for himself how things were at the store, did Mark get a call from Woodside that would delay opening this morning? Did that qualify as irony or just lousy luck? Mark wasn't even sure why he'd been asked to come up to the school.

"Is Vicki sick?" he'd asked as soon as the woman on the phone said she was calling from Woodside.

"No, sir. We don't need you to pick up your daughter. Principal Morgan just needs to speak with you."

The new principal, Shay Morgan. Mark had received the same cheerful letter of introduction as the other Woodside parents, but he'd never met Shay face-to-face. Maybe this wasn't such bad luck after all. He'd been meaning to talk to her anyway about the Fitness Fair.

Before he disconnected the call he asked, more as a parental reflex than an actual concern, "Vicki's not in trouble, is she?" His daughter had been eerily well behaved since his wife died. Aside from her growing exasperation that Mark showed no signs of remarrying, she rarely fussed or challenged any of the rules. Rosy-cheeked Mrs. Norris said she was a dream to babysit for: "So quiet you hardly know she's in the house."

Instead of promptly assuring him that Vicki hadn't broken any rules, the secretary said primly, "You'll have to take that up with the principal." Then she hung up, leaving him perplexed for the duration of his fifteen-minute drive.

As it had in the past, walking through the school's front doors gave him a twinge, reminding him of how much it had stung, after Jess's death, to bring Vicki here on her very first day of kindergarten without her mother there to see it or help her get ready. Mark didn't often find himself on campus, except for periodic performances or the August orientation held each year so that students could meet their teachers for the first time. On those occasions, he was usually part of a noisy crowd. This morning, the front hallway was quiet. The only person he passed was a woman who appeared to be signing in her tardy son. Recognizing her as someone who'd shopped at the store before, Mark offered a small finger wave. Inexplicably, the woman smothered a giggle and glanced away sharply.

Oookay. Dismissing her strange behavior, Mark turned in to the main office. The school secretary, Roberta Cree, stood at the copy machine, feeding paper into the tray. Even though he'd seen Roberta before, he was struck anew by how short she was. Over the phone, she was much taller.

The secretary dipped her chin by way of greeting. "Mr. Hathaway. I'll let the principal know y—"

"Mr. Hathaway?" A blonde poked out of the office behind the front counter. "Mark Hathaway? I'm Shay Morgan."

Wow. Mark didn't recall any school principals looking like that during his childhood. Was she unusually young for a principal, or had his perspective of age simply adjusted now that he himself was an adult? Even without the added height of her black boots, she would be tall for a woman, and she was noticeably curvy beneath a soft aqua sweater that matched her eyes.

Unfortunately, those blue-green eyes were narrowing at him in displeasure.

Had he been caught ogling? It had been so long since he'd ogled that he really wasn't sure.

"I didn't mean to stare," he defended himself. "You're just not what I expected. I guess I'm so used to seeing Principal Ridenour come out of that office, and you're, uh…not him." Physically, it was hard to imagine how she could be any more unlike the stout, balding former principal.

"So I've been told," she said with a tight smile.

She ushered him into her office and shut the door, indicating one of the padded chairs that sat around a small round table. "Thank you for coming up to the school so quickly. It had been my intention to discuss this on the ph—" She broke off, frowned and started over. "I'm glad you're here, Mr. Hathaway. We need to talk about Vicki. Are you, by any chance, aware of an email that your daughter sent?"

"My daughter? That's impossible. Aside from the fact that she obviously doesn't have an email account, she never uses my computer without close supervision."

Shay—Principal Morgan—settled into one of the other chairs. She crossed her legs, displayed to flattering effect beneath her black skirt and thin hose. It caught him by surprise that he even noticed. Over the years, many women had come into the store, some of them athletic and, he supposed, quite pretty. But he'd have better luck describing what any one of them had purchased than what she looked like. Feeling off balance, it took him a moment to focus on what the principal was saying.

"A number of parents forwarded me this." She pushed a sheet of paper toward him.

Curious, he picked it up and glanced at the subject heading. *From Victoria Hathaway?*

"This is my sister-in-law's email address. Vicki…" He trailed off, recalling how pleased he and Dee had been that Vicki and Bobby were getting along so well. During the past two family dinners, the kids had shut themselves in the study with no discernible bickering or tattling. *Which should have been enough to make you suspicious, dummy.* "Vicki has a cousin who must have helped her. She wouldn't know how to send an email by herself."

"Bobby Riggs, Dee's son?" Shay nodded. "Earlier this week, I presented him with a trophy from the council-level science fair. Clearly a smart boy. It makes sense that Vicki would have dictated her letter—the punctuation and spelling are far above the normal first-grade level."

With growing trepidation, Mark began to read.

My name is Victoria Hathaway. People call me Vicki. I am six years old and in the first grade at Woodside Elementary school. I am the only girl in my class who doesn't have a mommy.

Mark's heart stuttered. He'd known Vicki was growing more resentful of her single parent status, but seeing her unhappiness articulated like that on the paper in front of him… He was shocked that, instead of trying to talk to him more about it, she'd decided to share it with the population of Woodside! What had Bobby been thinking to help her with this?

My daddy is Mark Hathaway. He is a good man, but a not so good cook. My mom went to heaven. He needs a new wife, but he never ever goes on dates.

Was it possible to keep one's face from turning red through sheer force of will? He kept his gaze locked on the humiliating paper in his hand and away from the lovely blonde who watched him silently.

I think my dad is shy. Can you help us? It will be Valentine's Day soon, and he is very lonely. If you are a lady who is not too old and don't already have a husband, maybe you could be Daddy's valentine. Please let him know if you would like him. He is gone at the store a lot, but he is fun when he is home. It would also be good if you have a dog. I really want one. But not as much as I want a mom.
Thank you,
Victoria Kathryn Hathaway

Mark was mortified. And aching for his daughter. And fully prepared to ground both her and her cousin for the rest of their natural lives. Well, she had tried to warn him that morning. *Don't worry, Daddy, I have a plan.* He was flooded with reactions, from grudging admiration of his daughter's problem-solving ingenuity—hell, maybe she could help brainstorm ideas on how to save the store—to renewed anger that his wife had been taken from them so young.

He heard his own rusty chuckle. In his struggle to formulate a response, he'd unconsciously chosen laughter. "Maybe I could just get her a puppy?"

"I'm not sure making jokes is the best way to handle this," the principal countered gently. "Your daughter obviously—"

"Have you even met my daughter?" he asked. Mark wasn't normally rude, but he was still reeling at the idea of Vicki feeling so desperate that she'd taken action behind his back. He always read the weekly notes from her teacher, Mrs. Frost, and Lord knew he'd listened to hours of advice from Dee because he accepted that his sister-in-law had Vicki's best interests at heart. But he resented the condescending tone from a woman who might not even recognize Vicki if she saw her.

Shay squared her shoulders, rigid in her chair. "I go into all of the classrooms, occasionally reading stories to the kids or picking a table to have lunch with, but no, I have not been individually introduced to your daughter. And, before you ask, no, I don't have any children of my own. What I do have are years of classroom experience working with kids and a Master of Education. I may be younger than Principal Ridenour, but I assure you I'm qualified for my job."

Mark shoved a hand through his hair, aware that he'd botched this meeting so far. "Of course you are, Ms. Morgan. I apologize. I got defensive because this is personal."

Her posture eased slightly, but her expression didn't

soften. "I understand why you would feel that way, but this email was sent to everyone on the PTA mailing list. I haven't spoken to Vicki yet, or her aunt, for that matter. I wanted to make sure that you, as the responsible parent, were fully aware of the situation first. But I am going to send out a concise email addressing the situation."

In other words, Mark translated, his "personal" matter had become quite public.

"Before we call her into the office, though," the principal added, "I wanted to talk with you for a few minutes. Are you aware that there's a community support group for single parents that meets in the school cafeteria the first and third Wednesday nights of every month?"

"I appreciate that you're trying to help, but I'm not going to give up another night with my daughter. Tuesday evenings she has ballet, and Friday, inventory at the store sometimes goes pretty late, so—"

"That would be the store mentioned in Vicki's letter, when she says you're away a lot? Mr. Hathaway, as someone who's never been married, I can't know precisely what it's like to lose a spouse. But I realize it must be very difficult for you and Vicki. Maybe this wasn't so much a plea for a new mom as a cry for more attention."

"Vicki knows how much I love her." *Doesn't she?* "I tell her every single day. She's the most… She's my world, Ms. Morgan." He recalled a promise he'd made to Jess, when they'd known how little time she'd had left. He'd told her that he'd love Vicki enough for both of them. Was he failing?

"I don't doubt that." Radiating sympathy, the principal laid her hand atop his on the table. Then she blinked, as if she were as surprised by the physical contact as he was. She withdrew immediately. "Maybe it would help if you supplemented your words with actions, with your time. The first-grade classes have already been on a couple of field trips this year. Were you able to chaperone any of those?"

"I have a store to run." This woman had no idea what kind of pressure he was under to keep the place afloat and to keep Vicki here in Braeden. Was he really being condemned as a bad father because he hadn't accompanied a bunch of six-year-olds to a petting zoo?

"You also have a daughter who needs you," she said. "There are numerous studies that show how much a child benefits, both emotionally and academically, when a parent is able to volunteer at the school."

Those studies weren't going to pay his mortgage. But he tamped down the sarcasm. If his showing up for the occasional field trip would help Vicki, he'd find a way to do it. But it seemed that Ms. Morgan had even bigger ideas.

She handed him a blue folder. "That contains information on different ways you can get involved in the classroom. We're always in need of parental support for our activities. Our fall book fair, normally a week long, only ran three days this year because we couldn't staff all of the available shifts. And the Campside Girls who've traditionally had their weekly troop meetings here had to disband this year because they couldn't find a leader."

"A shame," he muttered. "I would have been happy to give the troop discounts on gear for—"

"Mr. Hathaway! We're discussing your daughter's well-being, not your store. Study the list I've given you.

There must be something on it that you're suited to, a way you can chip in and show Vicki that she's just as important to you as your job."

Maybe the two could dovetail—his principal-mandated community service and his promise to Bennett to boost business.

"Actually, it's a funny coincidence," Mark said, flashing her a smile. He tried for charm but it was difficult to gauge whether or not he succeeded. "I wanted to talk to you about getting involved with Woodside this spring."

"Really?" Her tone was suspicious.

"Honest. I know Woodside's hosting that Fitness Fair and as you may know, at Up A Creek, we—"

"That's the name of your store?"

"It's the store I manage, yes. I'm not the owner." And if he didn't find a way to boost profits enough to appease the owner, then—

"Mr. Hathaway, I believe you are missing the point." Her tone was wooden. "Your daughter needs you."

This judgmental blonde didn't think he was aware of that fact every second of every day? Vicki needed him to braid hair, which he couldn't do, and provide dinner, which he usually messed up; the matter-of-fact criticism in her email that he was a *not so good cook* stung more than he would have predicted. But she also needed him to provide food and shelter and the clothes she seemed to outgrow every other week.

The responsibility had been weighing heavily on his shoulders lately. Now, with Shay Morgan poking at his flaws, he wanted to yell that he was doing the best he could. Ironically, it was the very fear that his words might be true that kept him silent.

What if this *was* the best he had to offer and it wasn't enough to truly keep his daughter healthy and happy?

He tightened his grip on the folder, sucking in his breath at the resulting paper cut. "I'll read everything in here and find a way to participate."

"Wonderful! I look forward to working with you," Shay lied unconvincingly. She sounded as if she'd rather be buried beneath a rock slide than deal with him again.

He could relate. That was pretty much how he felt about her right now, too.

As SHE WAITED ALONE IN her office for Mark Hathaway's return, Shay took a moment to compose herself. They'd asked Roberta to call for Vicki via the classroom intercom system, but Mrs. Frost had answered that the class was outside with the gym teacher and that it would take a few minutes to find Vicki and escort her to the office. Meanwhile, Mark had stepped outside to phone his store—the cell reception was lousy in the school—so he could let his employee know it would be at least another half an hour before he returned to work. He'd excused himself with a note of challenge in his voice, as if expecting Shay to come down on him for being a diligent boss.

She sighed, staring sightlessly at her computer monitor. *Well, you've handled this like a real pro.*

No doubt startled by his daughter's attempts to engineer his love life, Mark Hathaway had been prickly throughout their meeting. It hadn't helped that instead of defusing the situation, Shay herself had felt defensive, unbalanced. Her original intention had been to phone the man and discuss Vicki's email, but Roberta had acted preemptively, summoning him to the office on Shay's behalf. Would their conversation have gone more smoothly if it hadn't been face-to-face?

Get a grip. He's hardly the first good-looking man you've ever met.

True, but she wasn't reacting just to Mark's tall, athletic build or the handsome face framed by inky-black hair. She was responding more to *his* reaction to her. The way his gaze had traveled over her in the front office... If she'd been out somewhere socially, instead of at a place of work where she was trying to establish her authority, the appreciation in those gray eyes would have made her shiver. And she hadn't missed his staring at her legs once they sat down together.

But despite the temptation to be flattered as a woman, she was annoyed as a professional. *You're not what I expected,* he'd said, comparing her to Principal Ridenour. Was Mark Hathaway one of those people who would underestimate her as a pretty face, too young and not up to the serious responsibilities of her job? He certainly wouldn't be the first. Her thoughts flickered from the mothers gathered outside her office this morning to her own father, but she shut down that line of contemplation. This morning was about little Victoria Hathaway, not Shay.

Sometimes this job called for deciding what was best for students as a whole, implementing policies that would affect the nearly three hundred kids at Woodside, but other days, it was far more personal, trying to help each child one at a time. And, as exasperating as her parents could sometimes be, Shay loved them both and couldn't imagine how difficult a time this was for the motherless first grader.

Though her door was open, Mark Hathaway rapped his fist against the doorjamb, looking tentative. "Just wanted to make sure I wasn't interrupting a phone call or anything," he said as he walked back into the office. Instead of regaining his seat, he stood behind the chair, shifting his weight.

"I asked Roberta to hold my calls until after we talked to Vicki. I figure she'll be unnerved enough without having to sweat it out while I'm talking to someone else. Barring any sudden emergencies on campus, you two have my undivided attention."

Frankly, Mark Hathaway probably had women's undivided attention no matter where he went. Now that she'd been able to put a face with the name, it was a bit surprising that this man "never ever" went on dates. Was his daughter exaggerating? Or was he still in mourning for his late wife?

Shay cleared her throat. "Mr. Hathaway, I apologize if this is a difficult question, but do you mind if I ask when your wife passed? I'm just trying to get a handle on Vicki's state of mind."

His knuckles tightened on the back of the chair. "About two years ago. She—"

"Ms. Morgan?" The secretary's voice crackled through the phone on Shay's desk. "I'm sending back Vicki Hathaway now."

"Thank you." Shay stood and returned to the table by the door so that they could all sit together.

A little girl who looked absolutely nothing like Mark appeared in the doorway. Judging from their facial features, one wouldn't even guess them related. Where his dark hair was silky, her ginger-colored hair was a profusion of curls. Shay's hair had always been naturally straight, requiring determined use of a curling iron and lots of hair spray to achieve any kind of body. Vicki Hathaway was adorable and, Shay suspected, probably a miniature of Mark Hathaway's late wife. Did it comfort him, seeing part of Mrs. Hathaway live on, or did looking at a version of her face make him miss her even more keenly?

Vicki's chin was bravely raised even though her lower lip quivered and her brown eyes were huge with trepidation. "Hi, Daddy."

Still standing, he turned to wrap an arm around his daughter's slim shoulder. "Hi, Bug."

"Would you like to sit down with us, Vicki?" Shay pointed to the empty seat between herself and Mark. "I'm Principal Morgan."

Vicki nodded solemnly.

"Do you know why your dad and I want to talk to you?" Shay asked softly.

Vicki slouched down in the chair. "B-because of the letter that Bobby and I—I mean, the letter *I* sent?"

Mark exhaled with a huff. "We already know your cousin was your partner in crime. This was his idea, wasn't it?"

"No." Despite her trembling lip, Vicki's expression was resolute when she swiveled her head to look at her father. "It was my idea to help you meet a nice lady. I had that idea even before Christmas. You're too shy, Daddy. You need my help! You and Aunt Dee and Pasture Jack—"

"Pastor Jack," her father corrected automatically.

"You all say we should help people, right?"

"Well, yes," Mark conceded, "but we have to be careful how we do it." He cast a beseeching glance in Shay's direction. The expression in his gray eyes clearly read *Help!* which, she had to admit, was enormously gratifying. This parent had gone from questioning just what she knew about his daughter to seeking out her expertise.

She cleared her throat. "Vicki, do you remember when that policeman visited the school last week and talked to us about 9-1-1? He said it was important to know your phone number and address but that we don't share that information with strangers."

Vicki nodded. "Wanna hear my phone number?"

"Maybe another time. Right now, I need you to understand that email addresses are a little like phone numbers. People want their privacy. When they filled in their personal contact information for the PTA, we promised that they would only get emails with official PTA updates. You and your cousin didn't have any right to use that mailing list. And I think you know that it was wrong to go behind your dad's back like that. Don't you?"

Vicki's gaze fell momentarily to her lap, where she was wringing her hands. But she made one last attempt to plead her case. "Do you think little girls should have a mommy?" She raised her head, hitting Shay with the full force of those chocolate-brown eyes.

Shay had worked with children for enough years to understand that the smart ones started trying to manipulate adults from an early age—testing the grown-ups around them and testing boundaries. To some extent, she was being played. Still, even if they were being exaggerated for effect, the pain and frustration in Vicki's small voice were real. Shay had the urge to scoop the girl into a hug.

But she hadn't become principal by letting children

wrap her around their little fingers—not even supercute, resourceful, motherless children. So she chose to answer Vicki's question with one of her own. "Do you think your mommy would have wanted you to do things that upset your dad or other adults?"

"No, ma'am," Vicki whispered.

"Can you promise me that nothing like this will happen again?" Shay asked gently.

"Yes. But *someone* has to do *something,*" she whined, foreshadowing what she was likely to sound like as a teenager.

"I know it's difficult not having your mother around," Shay said. "But you still have a dad who loves you very much."

"Very," Mark interjected, taking his daughter's hand. "And he wants to spend even more time with you."

"He does?" Vicki whipped her head around, looking to her dad for confirmation.

The first grader seemed blatantly skeptical, which proved Shay's earlier point. Part of this mom search probably stemmed from the little girl's feeling neglected. If Mark made a concerted effort to be more involved in his daughter's life, not only would it be good for her emotional well-being, it would save him a lot of trouble in the long run.

Shay nodded emphatically, addressing Vicki but shooting a pointed glance toward Mark. "Yep. He's going to find some ways to help out at the school."

"Just like Lorelai's mom," Vicki said excitedly.

Oh, let's hope not. One Carolyn Moon was more than enough for any administrator.

Shay suppressed a grimace, instead offering a smile of encouragement. "Before I send you back to class, I need you to make us one more promise. You and your cousin used those email addresses without permission and what you did was a violation of privacy. I need you to write an apology."

Vicki scrunched up her face. "I can't spell *violation!*"

"I'll help you, just like I help with your homework," Mark said. He said it so quickly, with a sidelong glance at the principal, that Shay felt like he was trying to redeem himself. The subtext of his declaration seemed to be *We read, we do math. See? I don't suck as a father.*

Shay experienced a twinge of guilt. Had she been too hard on him earlier? She shook off the thought, deciding not to second-guess herself. After all, her tough love approach had worked. She'd won a grudging concession from him to be more involved with his daughter and Vicki already looked delighted by that idea.

By the time they wrapped up their conference, Mark had promised that the principal would have Vicki's written apology in hand by Monday morning. And Vicki had sworn—"cross my heart"—that she would never send out another unauthorized email again. Shay bid them both a warm farewell, adding that she was always available if they needed to talk.

Once they were gone and she'd sat back down at the computer, she couldn't help the unbidden thought that if Vicki had *really* wanted to make her Valentine email effective, she should have attached a JPEG image of her father.

FOR HIS MEETING WITH the principal, Mark had turned off his cell phone. As he crossed the frigid parking lot toward his car, he switched the phone back on and discovered that he had four voice-mail messages from Dee.

He dialed her number, unsurprised when she answered on the first ring.

"I am never letting Bobby near a computer again," she said immediately. "I'm serious. His days of commandeering my PC for homework purposes are *over*. I'll buy him a typewriter, an abacus and an encyclopedia set."

Mark laughed. "Far be it from me to tell you how to raise your kid, but tossing the boy back into the Stone Age might be overkill. Grounding him and making him apologize should do it. In fact, Vicki and I just met with Principal Morgan, who wants a written apology on her desk by Monday morning. You'll probably be getting a call from her."

"Oh, Mark—the two of you got summoned to the principal's office? You just *wait* until Robert Joseph gets home," she said, annoyed enough to use her son's full name. "I had a doctor's appointment first thing this morning and was running late for car pool, so I didn't even check email before I left. He was safely at school before I found out what he'd done. What were those children thinking?"

Her question, although probably rhetorical, was followed by a deeply awkward pause as they both acknowledged what the scheming duo had been thinking. They'd been reasoning that kids deserved two parents and that Vicki missed her mother. And that Mark had failed abysmally when it came to rejoining the dating world of singles.

"As your daughter pointed out, Valentine's Day is right around the corner," Dee said. "I don't suppose there's anyone special you were interested in ask—"

"Not you, too!" Mark protested. If his daughter

broadcasting his supposed romantic ineptitude to hundreds of people was the most embarrassing thing that had ever happened to him, then discussing his love life with his late wife's big sister ran a close second.

"Is it because of Jess?" Dee asked quietly. "If you're not ready for another relationship, I understand. But if something else is keeping you from… We spend a lot of time together and there are pictures of her all over my house. I wouldn't ever want you to feel guilty about seeing someone else. Jess would want you to be happy, and Frank and I would be completely supportive if that's what you wanted."

"It isn't," Mark said. "Not right now, anyway. You know that things haven't been going too well at the store? The owner, Bennett Coleridge, is in town for the weekend. He's thinking about shutting me down, Dee."

She sucked in her breath. "Oh, no."

"So I'm a little preoccupied right now. Besides, a woman in my life shouldn't be a Band-Aid. If I go out with someone, it should be because we're interested in each other as two adults, not because I need her in order to bond with my own daughter."

Maybe the principal had been right today, damn it. While he resented the implication that he wasn't there for his daughter, maybe he *wasn't* there for her in the ways that made the most sense to a six-year-old. Obviously it was imperative that he provided for her, but maybe—in her view—it was equally imperative that he watched some of her ballet lessons or read to her class.

"Vicki and Bobby were sneaking off to do this," he continued, "and I never had an inkling that she was up to something." When she'd flat out admitted this morning that she had "a plan," his brilliant parenting strategy had been to dismiss what she was trying to tell him. *Dumbass.* "Before I think about any romantic relationships, I should probably strengthen my relationship with my daughter."

"All right. But you know if you ever do want to take someone out for the evening, we're happy to babysit."

"Thank you. You and Frank have been amazing. I don't think I tell you that enough, but we're so blessed to have you." Even Bobby had arguably acted out of love for his cousin. Mark couldn't fathom what it would be like for himself and Vicki to start over from scratch somewhere else, without their invaluable support network.

I won't let that happen, he vowed to himself as he disconnected the call. He would simply redouble his efforts to keep the store open. But he wouldn't let those efforts stop him from being the father that Vicki deserved.

Chapter Three

"Oh, it's you." Since the store was currently deserted, Mark's words carried.

From just beneath the bell that jangled to announce patrons, six-foot-five Cade Montgomery raised his eyebrows. "Dude, stop falling all over yourself with elation whenever you see me. People will talk."

"Sorry, didn't mean to sound unhappy that you're here," Mark said. "I was just hoping…"

"That I was a paying customer?" Cade commiserated. In years past, the dark-haired bear of a man had earned a full-time living with guided rafting excursions, but in the current economy, he had to supplement that income with carpentry odd jobs.

"Yeah."

"It's the middle of a weekday," Cade pointed out. "People are either at work or at lunch. You'll get more business tomorrow."

"I know." But would it be enough business? Since Mark had reached the store after this morning's meeting at Woodside, he'd been consulting vendor catalogs, trying to decide if he could cut costs by dropping certain brands that weren't selling well or switching distributors.

"Speaking of lunch. I was in the area delivering some

shelves to a client and swung by to see if you wanted to grab a burger with me."

"But that would mean closing the store for an hour."

Cade glanced meaningfully at the reversible Open sign hanging in the window; the back featured an adjustable clock face. "Gee, if only you had one of those signs that said something like 'Will Return In….'"

Mark rolled his eyes. "Smart-ass. I was planning to work through lunch because I missed some time this morning. I got called into an unexpected meeting with the new principal at Woodside."

"About that Fitness Fair?"

"No, about Vicki." *The tiniest matchmaker.* Mark had seen movies where children of single parents schemed to get their folks together. But those were always specific matches—one man, one woman. His overachieving daughter had tried to hook him up with the entire damn PTA!

"Vicki? Is she winning an award or something?" Cade asked, unmistakable affection in his voice.

"Not unless the school gives out awards for most inappropriate use of email."

Cade's brows shot up. "Don't follow."

Mark sighed. "Come on. Let's get lunch, and I'll tell you all about it."

RECAPPING THE MORNING'S ego-bruising events for his friend's entertainment did not improve Mark's mood. Even though it had been Cade's idea to go eat, the man had mostly ignored his bacon burger in favor of laughing at Mark.

"I had no idea your daughter was so proficient with

the internet," Cade said, still chortling. "If I'd known, I would have friended her on Facebook. Hey, think she could talk me through a problem I've been having with Outlook?"

"Glad you find this so hilarious," Mark groused.

"And you don't? You have to admit, what she did was really cute."

"Says the man who wasn't getting lectured by Principal Morgan first thing this morning."

"That's right, I remember hearing a new principal moved here from the opposite end of the school district. What's she like, the female version of Ridenour?" Even though Cade didn't have any young relatives at the elementary school, it was a small town and everyone had at least a passing acquaintance with Jonathan Ridenour, one of Braeden's most involved citizens until his heart attack.

At the idea of comparing Shay to Ridenour, Mark finally cracked a grin. Cade was a good guy, but a bit of a hound dog. He'd dated at least half of the attractive single women in the tricounty area yet had no idea that a beautiful blonde had recently taken up residence nearby. "No, she's not much like Ridenour. Younger, for one thing."

"Makes sense. Why replace him with someone who would just retire in another year or two?"

Mark frowned, remembering his encounter with Shay. "And I think Jonathan would have been slower to assume it was my fault. He's got kids, grandkids. He understands that sometimes they just… Do you think I'm a bad father?"

"Hell, no. You adore that little girl. But you know enough to tell her when it's time to go to bed and not give her whatever she wants just because she throws a fit. Not that I've ever seen her throw one," Cade qualified. "Of course, that's probably just because you're such a good dad you've taught her better manners than that. Look, don't ask me about parenting. What do I know? Talk to your sister-in-law if you're really worried."

That made Mark feel better. After all, no one questioned that Dee was a great parent, even though her son had been Vicki's accomplice. Somewhat mollified, he admitted, "It's not that I think Principal Morgan is wrong, per se, about my getting involved. I just don't think she can fully appreciate the pressure I'm under as a single dad. She's never been in the parenting trenches herself."

Cade swiped a fry through some ketchup. "You think maybe she's bitter? Got into teaching because she loves kids but never had any of her own? Maybe she's jealous of people with families."

Mark opened his mouth to correct his friend's misconception that Shay was a woman well past her prime, but the waitress came back to refill their drinks and Cade spent the next few minutes flirting with her. Once she was gone, conversation turned to Mark's store and his idea about contacting nearby lodges and resorts like Hawk Summit.

"You know, there's actually been some buzz about trying to reopen the campsite on the edge of Braeden," Cade said. "If that happened, it could indirectly benefit you. Stop by the town meeting next week, make a case for why it would be good for all of us."

"Maybe." Mark suspected he could get Dee to babysit, but if he was going to publicly address his fellow towns-people, he needed to come up with something convincing.

I don't want my poor kid to have to move probably wasn't the most effective argument. Then again, thanks to her email, the general public was already aware that she was unhappy. Surely they wouldn't want to further traumatize the motherless, dogless child.

"And you could always check out some of those SBA classes offered through the county seat," Cade added. "Registration fees are minimal and even though you aren't technically a small business owner, they might have some economical marketing tips you can implement. The more professionally defined your prospective partnership when you approach places like Hawk Summit, the better the chances they'll accept."

Mark shook his head, chuckling. "You may have the largest collection of flannel shirts in North Carolina, but I swear you wore a suit in a previous life."

"Who, me?" Cade sipped his soda, avoiding the implied question. He'd only been in Braeden for four or five years and rarely talked about where he was from or what had brought him there. "Dude, I build cabinets in my garage. But I did date an MBA once. Maybe I picked up some pointers from her."

As they exited the Burger Shop, automatically bracing against the biting wind, Cade suggested, "Maybe *you* should date an MBA. Totally solve all your problems—get some informal consulting on the store and make Vic happy. Don't you think the kid deserves a mother figure?"

Mark ground his back teeth together. "Some of us have an ethical problem using women."

"I don't 'use' anyone!" Cade sounded legitimately offended. "I may not be looking for anything serious, but that doesn't mean I'm not fond of the women I spend time with."

"Sorry. But don't you think trying to appease my six-year-old would be a pretty crappy reason to ask someone out?"

"Fair enough." Cade unlocked his truck. "So ask someone out for you. I've never busted your chops about living like a monk—statistically speaking, I'm probably dating your share of ladies as well as mine—but it's been about two years."

"Are you suggesting there's a statute of limitations on how long I love my wife?" Mark growled.

"Of course not. If you're still carrying a torch, that's your business. I'm just saying…if the problem is you're nervous about getting back on the horse—"

Mark snorted.

"So to speak." Cade flashed a grin. "Allowing more time to slip by isn't going to ease your nerves. It's like jumping in a pool. Don't stand on the edge staring down into the deep end, just close your eyes and do it."

Cade turned the keys in the ignition and neither man spoke as they pulled out of the parking lot. Mark couldn't help tossing his friend's advice around his head, though.

After a few minutes, he blurted, "I'll always love Jess, but I think it would be possible to love someone else, too. In theory."

"But in practice?"

"Jessica and I met in high school." He'd only kissed three or four girls before he'd started dating his future wife. "We were together a long time. After the first year she'd been gone, I felt obligated to try again. I went on a few dates over the course of three months and they were so awful that I quit. What's the point of trying to find room for it in my schedule when it was only making everyone involved miserable? One woman reached over during a movie and held my hand wrong."

Cade snickered. "How can you hold hands *wrong?*"

"It's like having a side of the bed, I guess, but with fingers. Shut up," Mark said when his friend continued to laugh at him. Okay, it sounded stupid when he tried to explain it out loud, but the truth was, he and Jess had fit seamlessly after so many years together. It wasn't just that when they held hands his thumb was always on the outside, it was everything.

On one of his ill-fated dates, he and the woman had gone by a drive-through restaurant to grab food for an outdoor concert and he'd reflexively asked the employee to leave the mayonnaise off her burger. Explaining that he was used to ordering for his late wife had done nothing to ease the first-date tension. Another time, he'd attempted a good-night kiss but they'd both leaned in on the same side, banging their noses together.

"I feel like one of those people who got the full-on amnesia, where they have to relearn everything from words to how to hold a spoon. It's so damn frustrating."

Cade considered this. "Maybe it's all in how you choose to look at it. Take me—learning all about a new woman is part of the fun. It's exciting. No two are alike."

That kind of "excitement" held little appeal for Mark. Besides, it wasn't just getting to know strangers that made dating difficult. He and Jessica had grown up together; in a lot of ways, she'd shaped the adult he became. Because he'd been blessed in finding the woman he wanted to be with so young, he'd never had experience with a breakup or how different women liked to be touched, the types of relationship lessons many guys learned by the time they finished college. When he was out with someone now, it wasn't only that Mark didn't know her, he felt like he barely knew himself.

"I admire your confidence with women, but not all of us can be Mr. Smooth," Mark said wryly. "Turns out, I'm more the stammering and second-guessing type."

"You don't know that! Jess clearly thought you were Prince Charming and I'll bet lots of other women would agree. Three or four awkward evenings in the course of your lifetime is hardly definitive proof that you suck at dating."

"How comforting. Look, if it will shut you up, I'll make you a deal. Drop the subject until April, when Coleridge makes a decision about the store. After that, if I'm still here, you can set me up with every single female you know."

"Every?" Cade laughed. "Better clear your summer calendar."

"I was being figurative, not literal. Just give me until April."

"Deal. But I'm not your problem. What kind of deal are you planning to make your daughter?"

Mark pinched the bridge of his nose. He definitely needed to follow Principal Morgan's advice—get more involved with Vicki, keep her busy and happily occupied with other aspects of her life. Because left to her own devices, by April she'd probably be going through the Braeden phone book, calling women individually to ask if they would be interested in dating her daddy.

WHEN MARK WALKED THROUGH the door leading in the house from the garage, Mrs. Norris looked up quizzically from her knitting at the kitchen table and Vicki, who appeared to be doing her homework, squealed with delight.

"Daddy!" She bolted out of her chair and barreled toward him. "Why are you home early?"

"I asked Roddy to come in at four-thirty instead of seven. He said that just this once, he can handle inventory by himself." Which meant that instead of sleeping in tomorrow, Mark would have to double-check the numbers in the morning, but it seemed like a fair trade-off in order to spend an extra evening reassuring his kid. "Is it okay with you that I'm here already?"

Nodding enthusiastically, she hugged him. But then she pulled away, biting her lower lip and glancing back toward Mrs. Norris. "We were gonna order a pizza for dinner."

"Sounds good to me." He extricated himself from his daughter enough to set his laptop case on the kitchen counter, then handed Mrs. Norris the envelope with her weekly paycheck. "Everything going okay here?"

"Vicki was no trouble whatsoever. We made cutout gelatin shapes for afternoon snack and read a chapter book together." The elderly woman grinned, her cloudy blue eyes suddenly flashing with an impishness that made her look far younger. "But your phone's been ringing a lot today. Took some mighty interesting messages for you."

Mark groaned. Were people calling to complain about Vicki's email…or to answer it? Surely the women of Braeden had more sense than that. Her letter had been a child's act of desperate whimsy, not a legitimate solicitation in the *Braeden Bugle* personal ads!

After Mrs. Norris had wished them both a great weekend and headed home, Mark sat in one of the kitchen chairs, studying his daughter. "Any hard homework tonight?"

She shook her head. "Not on Fridays. Just a word search on tall tales and legends. But I can't find Paul Bunyan."

"Really? That's strange. Isn't he like ten feet tall?"

After looking at him blankly for a second, she giggled. "The *word,* Daddy. I can't find the word *Paul Bunyan.*"

"Ah." He set up his laptop as she continued her search, wondering if he still got credit for coming home early to be with his daughter even if he planned to work tonight.

A few minutes later, she triumphantly declared, "Finished!"

"Way to go." He waited until she'd put the sheet back into her red Return to School folder. "Part of the reason I came home early is because we need to talk about some stuff, Vicki-bug."

Her face fell. "Am I still in trouble?"

"Well, we need to work on that apology you promised Principal Morgan, and—"

"She's pretty," Vicki interrupted.

Mark frowned, not sure if was just a random observation—which he'd discovered were not uncommon from six-year-olds—or if she had a specific purpose for saying so. "Yeah, I guess she is."

"I thought principals were scary. And mean, like in

that cartoon Bobby watches. Our principal is a lot more better."

They'd had the "cartoons are not accurate" discussion a year and a half ago when Vicki tried to color a tunnel on the wall with black marker. "I'm sure Ms. Morgan likes you and the other kids. Why else would she get a job at a school?"

"I like her, too. Did you like her, Daddy?"

Not particularly. But that was a knee-jerk reaction to her criticism, not the whole truth. The woman was undeniably attractive, but beyond that, he'd been touched by the empathy in her voice when she asked about his wife and he'd admired the way Shay had handled Vicki. She'd addressed the situation with the exact right combination of kind understanding and sternness.

"I thought that she had some good ideas," he said neutrally. "For instance, she suggested that I find ways you and I can spend more time together. I need your help with that. I know you like ballet, but I can't see Daddy in a tutu."

She giggled, the noise so sweet and purely joyful that it warmed him inside.

"So what other activities do you like? Anything we could do together? You haven't pulled out your bike in a long time. Maybe I could fix up mine and we could go for rides."

Her smile faded as she squirmed in her seat. "You remember one time I fell down and cut my leg? I had my helmet on and pads but I still got hurt."

Life was definitely like that sometimes—even when people took all the smart safety precautions, they could find themselves flat on the pavement with the wind knocked out of them, shocked by the pain they didn't see coming. He remembered getting Jess's diagnosis like it was yesterday. How could it possibly be so bleak when she was so damn young?

Mark swallowed. "I'm sorry you got hurt, but don't you think you might want to try again someday?"

"Someday," she said unenthusiastically, not meeting his gaze.

He started to tell her that the longer she put it off, the more difficult it would become to face her fears, but that reminded him uncomfortably of the lecture Cade had given him today about dating, so he changed the subject. "You know, your cousin Bobby is in science club and plays soccer after school. Are there any sports or clubs you want to join?"

"There was." She frowned. "But not anymore. Valerie in my class was gonna be a Campside Girl. Her big sister told her it was real fun and Valerie and me wanted to join but there weren't enough mommies." She heaved a colossal sigh that spoke volumes about the ongoing injustice of her world. "If I had a mommy, maybe she coulda been a Campside leader."

"You have a daddy," he reminded her. "Is there a rule that says troop leaders have to be female?"

"I don't know. I'm just a kid."

"Well, I'll check into it," he promised her. "Maybe it's not too late to put together a troop for the spring." And even if it was, Vicki would see her father making an effort on her behalf. "Now, how about we work on your apology letter and order that pizza?"

"Can we eat it on TV trays and watch a DVD? Pleeease."

If they put in one of her DVDs, he could keep her company in the living room while simultaneously doing a little research on his computer and working on his remarks for Thursday's town council meeting. When guilt pinged him over working during their "quality time" together, he decided that while he was at his laptop, he'd also see if Mrs. Frost's latest email was still in his inbox. It seemed as if the teacher sent out weekly requests for someone to come be the "mystery reader" or assist with a special in-class project.

Mark nodded at his daughter. "Dinner and a movie, you got it."

She beamed in awed excitement, as if she were in the presence of a superhero. As he made plans to hang out with his best girl, he told himself this was a great way to spend a Friday night. He pushed aside the conversations he'd had today with Dee and Cade and denied the occasional pang that indicated something was missing from his life.

Chapter Four

It took a true friend to call at an ungodly hour on a Saturday morning and bully you into braving freezing temperatures, all in the name of your physical health. Shay had even tried arguing, "It can't set us back that much to miss one workout."

"Might I remind you," Geneva said cheerfully, "that we promised not to let each other wiggle out of this? We set goals and a schedule and you were the one who said it was crucial to stick to it, make it a habit. It would be easy to rationalize skipping it once, and then once would become twice and—"

"I got it, I got it. I'll be there in twenty minutes," Shay said.

Although Geneva's house had a much smaller master bedroom, living room and kitchen than the newer one-and-a-half-story brick home Shay was renting, Geneva was the one with a finished basement, one section of which she'd converted into an exercise room.

When Shay had first come to Braeden to sign her rental agreement—with an option to buy, assuming she was named principal for the long term—she'd done a tour of the town to find the essentials: the grocery store, a decent place to buy shoes and a bookstore. That was how she'd met Geneva Daniels, proprietor of Book 'Em Daniels. Most bookshops these days had in-store coffee counters, but Geneva's small coffee-serving bakery was Hawaiian themed. She specialized in macadamia cookies, pineapple upside-down muffins and Kona blend coffee. The two women had become immediate friends over a plate of Geneva's coconut-crème tarts.

Of course, Geneva had noted that taste-testing her tropical desserts was taking a toll on her dress size and Shay admitted that she was not as in shape as she would prefer, either. Although scheduling time for fitness wasn't always simple, when she was active she was more energetic and more mentally focused—both attributes she needed in her mission to impress the parents and faculty at Woodside. Her position as principal was only guaranteed through the end of the year, but if she did a good job, it would become hers permanently.

After she knocked on Geneva's front door, a large bottle of water in her other hand, her friend greeted her with, "Aerobic warm-up followed by weight training, or high-intensity kickboxing?"

Shay slid free of her bulky winter jacket and hung it on the coatrack. "Maybe I should work out some latent aggression with kickboxing. That will probably make me a better dinner guest at my parents' tomorrow. All I want is to hear how everyone's doing and enjoy my mom's lasagna without sitting through a critique of my life choices. Is that too much to ask?" At the thought of her father's unintentional patronization and her mother fussing over her, Shay felt primed and ready for an hour of uppercuts and roundhouse kicks.

Geneva made a sympathetic noise. "Been there. As the only unmarried Daniels sibling—out of five, you understand—I was the main cause for parental despair. But then my older brother got divorced and my nephew in Chicago took up graffiti and suddenly I was off the hook." She paused, looking sheepish. "Tell me I didn't just sound happy that my brother's marriage fell apart and my nephew is now tagging."

Shay followed her friend downstairs, chuckling. "Well, you're a bad person, we knew this."

Geneva smirked over her shoulder. "It's what makes me such a fun friend."

"Which is why I love you in spite of your sadistic insistence that we exercise."

When they got downstairs, Geneva admitted, "It might take me a minute to find the right workout. I have a bad habit of not always putting DVDs in the right cases when I'm done with them."

While she waited, Shay began stretching and sent up a silent prayer that tomorrow's dinner party would only include her immediate family. Her mother had ambushed her once last year by inviting the single son of some quilting club friend. And Shay had been in a particularly bad mood that night. She'd just found out that her fellow assistant principal at the middle school where she worked was being promoted because their principal was moving up to a job in the superintendent's cabinet.

"We were equally qualified and I've been at that school longer than he has!" she'd complained to her mother while she put ice in all the glasses.

"Look at it from their perspective," Pamela Morgan had said calmly. "You're a relatively young female. It's easier to replace a teacher on maternity leave than the principal! You remember when I was teaching at Grossman and our principal never came back because she decided to stay home with the baby? It caused—"

"I'm not having a baby in the near future." Shay had smacked the plastic ice cube tray down on the counter. "I'm not even married!"

"Believe me, I know." Her mother had lowered her voice to a whisper, cutting her gaze toward the dining room. "But you don't have to be single forever. If you'd just give Bradley a chance..."

In the middle of a hamstring stretch, Shay found herself suddenly recalling Mark Hathaway. She felt a twinge of unexpected kinship with the man. Now that she stopped to think about it, they were in a similar boat, each being pressured by family who loved them to "remedy" their single status. *I should just be happy that my mom doesn't have access to the PTA mailing list.*

"Hey, boss, you might want to come out here," Roderick Mitchell said from the doorway of Mark's cramped office on Saturday afternoon. "I, uh, could use your assistance."

Mark glanced at the older man in surprise. Besides himself, Roderick Mitchell and Keesha Lewis were the store's only full-time employees. Mark also employed several part-timers and seasonal help around the Christmas holidays and in the summer, although he'd fired one part-time clerk for being rude to customers and never replaced him. Roddy, now retired from the military, was basically the second-in-command, closing on the nights Mark didn't. It was rare for the unflappable soldier to need help.

Mark knew that the other guy working today, Ed,

was away for his lunch hour. "Please make my day and tell me we're so swamped with customers that you can't check them all out."

"Um…there are about half a dozen people in the store. Female people," Roderick added. "And most of them have asked if you're here."

Mark's stomach lurched. "Are you kidding? Did Cade put you up to this?"

"No, sir. Although maybe he put the women up to it. Lord knows he has a way with the ladies."

Recalling the odd way divorced Tara Butcher had giggled this morning when Mark had explained the differences between different brands of sleeping bags, he accepted the reality of the situation. "Actually, we have my daughter to thank for this." With a resigned sigh, Mark accompanied Roddy onto the display floor.

As Roddy had estimated, there were only seven women—hardly enough to form a crowd. But it was notable that all the customers in the sporting goods store were female and that more than one of them seemed… overdressed for the occasion.

Lydia Fortnaut was the closest to him, and she immediately waved him over to where she stood by the fishing gear. "Yoo-hoo, Mark? I was hoping you could advise me on what works best at the lakes in this area. My sons used to fish with their father, before he ran off with his chiropractor's receptionist, damn his cheating black heart, and I thought maybe I could take up fishing, that it would give us a way to relate. I'm sure you understand the trials of being a single parent."

"Happy to help," he said. "We have lots of great equipment for people just starting out, but to clarify, you do know that fishing is prohibited most places around here until at least March?"

"Yes, but basketball season is in full swing," a brunette in a tight-fitting sweater interrupted. "And my Anthony…"

The twenty minutes passed in something of a blur as Mark fielded questions from three divorced moms, a woman who had nieces and nephews just his Vicki's age, and one marathon runner who managed to work into the conversation that she'd never had children but wasn't averse to being a mother one day.

"Wow," Roddy said, once the store was empty again. He stood at the cash register looking shell-shocked. "What the hell was that? Not that I'm complaining. We just sold ankle supports, water bottles, an air pump, a camping lantern, sunglasses, fishing lures, a tackle box and two fifty-dollar rods. That Lydia Fortnaut must want you bad."

Before Mark could explain what had precipitated the sudden rise in female clientele, Roddy snapped his fingers.

"We should institute a ladies' night at the store! I can't speak for Ed, but I'm willing to work in just a bow tie and jeans if that would help."

"I did not need that mental image," Mark complained.

"Hey, I may be knocking on fifty, but this body is in great shape. I haven't lost my marine discipline."

"Vicki desperately wants a mother," Mark said.

"Understandable for a little girl. Hell, there were times when I was overseas, a grown man and an armed solider, and wanted my mama. What did she do, ask all her little friends to send any single moms your way?"

"No, she sent an email to most all the parents at her elementary school saying that I was in need of a Valentine." Mark narrowed his eyes. "You laugh, you're fired."

"Yes, sir." Then Roddy bent down, placing his head on his folded arms, and laughed so hard the entire counter shook.

NEED MORE COFFEE. IT WAS a gray Monday morning, and although Shay had made it to work early, her brain seemed to have slept in and stayed home. She'd twice screwed up the prerecorded message that was supposed to go out through the school's automated phone system, reminding parents of third through fifth graders about the significance of the upcoming standardized testing. *Heck with it.* She had to leave the building soon anyway for a district meeting about a change this spring in how transfer requests were handled. Maybe she should go now, stop for an espresso on the way and try recording her "important message from your principal" when she returned.

Just as she'd reached in the lower desk drawer for her purse, her phone buzzed.

"Ms. Morgan? Are you available to see Victoria Hathaway? She says she's supposed to bring you something."

Vicki's note of apology. Shay had completely forgotten about it, although she'd been understandably distracted since her brother's unexpected announcement last night. Bastien had informed his family that he not only had a girlfriend—someone he'd met when she was visiting a friend in the hospital—he was planning to propose soon. *Propose!*

"Ms. Morgan?" The static-tinged connection of the aged intercom did nothing to mask the impatience in Roberta's voice.

Right, Vicki Hathaway. "Send her in." Shay admonished herself to focus but she couldn't help once again reliving her brother's startling declaration, as she had several times throughout her sleepless night.

"I didn't want to tell you about her at first because I wasn't sure how serious we were. Then I was half-convinced something might go wrong with our relationship, as if it were too good to be true." Perpetually confident Bastien had actually sounded nervous. *"But it's been perfect. She's perfect. Not in the sense that she has no flaws—I'm not an idiot—but in the sense that she's a perfect match for me. I would have brought her with me tonight except that she's at a user meeting in Vegas, but she can't wait to meet all of you."*

Naturally, all of the Morgans had been thrilled for him.

But tempering Shay's joy was the slightest sense of betrayal. Up until now, whenever her parents started in on her about being single, she could point out that her older brother was just as single. When their mother had gone to find a celebratory bottle of wine, Shay had entertained one petty second where she regretted covering for Bastien when he broke curfew at seventeen. *If I'd known he was going to do this to me twenty years later...*

Shaking off both last night's events and the rules her oh-so-perfect brother had surreptitiously broken when they were kids, Shay pasted a welcoming smile on her face for Vicki Hathaway.

"Good morning," she greeted the girl, coming around her desk to sit at the small conference table.

Vicki approached nervously, reminding Shay of Dorothy Gale coming to see the great Oz. "Good morning. Daddy said to bring you my a-pol-o-gy." She pronounced the word very slowly, as if it was something she'd been practicing and still hadn't quite mastered. "We worked hard on it."

"I'm glad to hear that," Shay told her, discreetly checking her watch. She still had a few minutes before she'd need to go. "Why don't you have a seat? If you don't mind, I thought maybe you could read me what you wrote."

"Okay," Vicki agreed after a moment's thought. She climbed into a chair, clutching the piece of notebook paper in her hand so hard it wrinkled. "I'm a good reader. I'm in the blue group in Mrs. Frost's class."

"That's wonderful," Shay praised. "Maybe you could even be a special helper and visit one of our kindergarten classes sometime, to read them a picture book?"

"I could?" Vicki sat up taller. "That would be cool!"

"I'll talk to Mrs. Frost about that," Shay promised. One of the concepts she really wanted to promote in the school was that of students helping each other. There were a few programs already in place designed to do that, but mostly it involved the fourth and fifth graders who had "book buddies" in the younger grades. It was worth trying out to see if some of the younger students could also succeed if given minor responsibilities.

"Do you want me to start now?"

Shay nodded her encouragement. "Whenever you're ready."

The little girl took a deep breath and launched into her letter so quickly that some of the words ran together. Shay had to replay a string in her mind to process what she was hearing. But after the first couple of lines, Vicki calmed down.

"Dear Principal Morgan and Woodside Elementary parents,
Last Friday, I sent an email to find my dad a Valentine because I think he is lonely and I want a mom. But it was not right to do that. I should respect privacy—Daddy helped me spell that—and not use other people's email. I should also not tell strangers about our home business and should not lie to my dad and tell him I am playing games with my cousin Bobby when we are up to no good. I will not do it again.
      Sincerely,
      Victoria Kathryn Hathaway."

No sooner had she finished than she added in a confidential tone, "My aunt Dee says Bobby is grounded from the computer until he is probably thirteen!"

Shay tried to bite back a grin. "Well, I'm glad the two of you have learned your lesson."

Vicki passed the paper to her. "I did. Next time I help Daddy find a date, I have to get his permission first."

Shay raised an eyebrow. "You mean you haven't given up on that?"

"Daddy says people should never give up," Vicki said brightly.

Oh, dear. "Maybe in this one instance it would be better to let it go," Shay cautioned. "Love between two people is… It happens in lots of different ways, but it can't be forced. And adult love is complicated. It might be hard for a little girl to help with it, even when she's a very smart, very persistent little girl."

Vicki was eyeing her intently. "Are you in love with a boy, Principal Morgan?"

"Uh, no."

"You sound like you know a lot about love."

Shay had the urge to backpedal like crazy and claim she didn't know the first thing about the subject, but that would negate her authority and the solid advice she'd just offered. "Well, some, I guess. Nobody knows everything about love."

"You can talk to my dad about love. Since you're a grown-up. That would be even more better than me helping."

"Just *better,*" Shay said absently. "We don't say *more better.* I'll tell you what, Vicki. As a principal, my job is to take care of things that have to do with class and learning and getting along with our friends at school. But I'm not really supposed to interfere much with—" what had the girl called it in her letter? "—home business. So I shouldn't say anything to your dad about dating. But what I can do is, if you ever have a question about school or a problem with something, I can help."

"Really?" Vicki's big brown eyes shone with gratitude and what looked like surprise.

"Really," Shay said firmly. "I care about you. I care about all the students at Woodside."

The girl cocked her head to the side. "That's just what my daddy said at home when we talked about you."

"The two of you talked about me?" *Oh, to have been a fly on the wall.* Shay knew that her conference with

Mark Hathaway had been a little bumpy, but despite the frustration she'd sensed from him, he obviously had the consideration not to bad-mouth her in front of his impressionable daughter. One would think parents would generally refrain from bashing other adults, especially school figures, in front of their children, but in Shay's experience, that wasn't always the case.

"I told Daddy you're not a scary principal. And we think you're pretty."

Shay felt foolish about the way her stomach flip-flopped. After all, she was only getting a six-year-old's side of the conversation—a six-year-old determinedly trying to fix up her father, at that. Who knew if Mark Hathaway really thought she was pretty?

Not that it would matter, even if he did. After all, Shay had until May to make her mark on this school and prove that she was an upstanding, dedicated principal. Somehow, she doubted that flirting with members of her PTA would go very far toward achieving that goal.

"You'd better get back to class now," she told Vicki.

"Okay." The girl stood but didn't move toward the door. "Principal Morgan?"

"Yes?"

Shay was unprepared for the way Vicki launched herself into a hug, wrapping her slender arms around Shay's shoulders.

"Thank you for liking me," Vicki whispered.

Shay would have told her *you're welcome,* but it was difficult to speak past the sudden lump in her throat.

Chapter Five

Mark's initial email to Hawk Summit resulted in a teleconference on Wednesday morning that was both promising and disappointing. He'd asked to speak to someone in the marketing department and had been startled to discover there wasn't one. After half an hour of candid conversation, the operations manager admitted that budget cuts had forced them to do away with the full-time, in-house department.

"It mostly falls to me, a part-timer with a background in PR and an intern who works without pay in exchange for college co-op credit and free skiing. What we can't do, we farm to an outside marketing firm."

The man was definitely interested in Mark's idea of cross-promotional deals, but hearing about Hawk Summit's struggles reinforced Bennett's suspicion that the resort was in no real shape to help the store. They'd also discussed some equipment that Hawk Summit could purchase through Up A Creek at a discount, which would help them both.

Congratulating himself on ending the teleconference in plenty of time to get to the elementary school, Mark grabbed his jacket and let Keesha know he was leaving.

"Going to read to my little girl's class," he said proudly.

"Sounds fun. What are you reading to them?"

Reading to them? Hell. That would explain the feeling that he'd forgotten something. Luckily, he had a box in the trunk of his car that should help. Dee had given him a bunch of books Bobby had outgrown, as well as some handheld electronic games that ran educational cartridges.

In the school parking lot, Mark pulled out the box and rifled through the books. Some appeared too old for his audience, some were nonfiction books about volcanoes and animal kingdom classifications that looked as if they might be too dry for read-aloud entertainment. But he struck gold with a slim chapter book that promised funny anecdotes about a grade school boy and his outrageous little brother, who was always getting them into wild scrapes. *Bingo.*

Book in hand, he took the front steps two at a time, appreciating that the weekend's predicted ice had never materialized.

According to the teacher's email, the procedure for mystery reader was that the parent checked in with the front office and Roberta Cree would announce via classroom intercom that a mystery guest had arrived. Then the teacher had all the kids close their eyes and put their heads down on their desks until the parent was situated in the chair at the front of the room and ready to start. Mark made a beeline for the office, nearly colliding with Principal Morgan. She was in a navy sweaterdress today that made her eyes look darker, with tan boots that hugged her calves.

Her mouth parted in surprise and she took a reflexive step back.

"Sorry," he said.

She gave a small smile. "Just so you know, there's no running in the halls, Mr. Hathaway."

He returned the smile. "Will it get me out of detention if I tell you I wasn't running, I was…power walking?"

Shay laughed, an unexpectedly low, throaty sound. Nothing like the periodic simpering giggles he'd heard over the weekend.

If he'd thought facing the women at the store on Saturday was awkward, it was nothing compared to church the next day. Two different ladies had approached him about joining the Sunday school class "specifically for adult singles. It's about Christian fellowship of course, but also companionship." If he wasn't mistaken, Patsy Elmer had *winked* when she'd added the last word. One of the members of the choir had caught up to him as he was leaving to give him a pan of brownies she'd baked from scratch. "For you and your adorable daughter. We should get her together with my Dylan sometime for a playdate. They're close in age."

"I see where your daughter gets her negotiating abilities," Shay told him. It was refreshing for a woman to bring up Vicki without having an ulterior motive. "She and I chatted on Monday when she brought me her letter. Job well done on that, by the way. But Mr. Hathaway…"

"Yes."

Shay bit her lip, looking indecisive, and Mark was shocked that he had such trouble tearing his gaze from her mouth. God, how long had it been since he'd really looked at a woman's mouth, really let himself think about—

"I should warn you," Shay said, "I don't think getting in trouble did anything to deter Vicki from wanting a mother."

Her words were as effective as a splash of cold water, making him forget not only his semi-inappropriate thoughts but that he was supposed to be on his way somewhere. "What is she up to now? Or do I even want to know?"

Shay laughed again, no doubt at the wariness in his tone that suggested his enterprising six-year-old was a mad scientist to be feared.

"She didn't share with me the schematics of her devious plan," the principal teased, "but she did mention something about how you taught her never to give up."

"Oh, sure." Mark lifted his free hand and rubbed his temple. "Everything I've tried to teach her since she was born, and *that's* the lesson she hones in on."

"She's a resilient, resourceful little girl. You should be very proud."

He felt a surge of paternal warmth. "Trust me, I am. And I'm taking your advice." He held up the chapter book. "I came to read to her class today, and I actually wanted to talk to you about another volunteer idea."

"Really? That's wonderful. I'm on my way to do a teacher evaluation and you're obviously expected in Mrs. Frost's class, but please call me later."

He nodded. "Look forward to talking to you."

The weird part was just how much he found himself looking forward to it.

SHAY MORGAN IS AN *intuitive genius*. Even if he hadn't been thrilled with her criticism when they first met,

Mark had never been more grateful for taking some-one's advice than he was at this moment. Although he'd predicted his daughter would be happy to see him—as far as he knew, kids didn't reach the stage where they pretended not to know their parents in public until at least age ten—he hadn't anticipated the depth of Vicki's joy. After he'd situated himself in the reading chair and Mrs. Frost had told the children that they could un-cover their eyes, Vicki had shrieked, "Daddy!" with the kind of delight he thought was reserved for events like a new puppy. Or even a pony. Yet his daughter's face was shining with more giddy surprise than she'd shown on Christmas morning, surrounded by new toys.

It was bolstering. Seeing how excited she was to have him around, he believed for the first time in a long time that maybe he would be enough. Maybe if he strengthened their bond, she could be content instead of constantly feeling the lack of a mother.

While his daughter's smile was definitely the bright-est, all of the children seemed pleased to have him there. Mrs. Frost, a round-faced woman with faded red hair and paint smears on her long denim skirt, commented that it was a rare treat for a dad to visit their classroom. Feeling like a superhero whose power was reading, he launched into the book. When he'd asked if any of the kids already knew it, they'd shaken their heads. He hadn't even passed the first page when he got his first laughs from the audience. He'd been lucky to have that box in his trunk and would have to remember to thank Dee later.

Finally, Mrs. Frost interrupted to tell the class they needed to prepare for their turn in the cafeteria—the first grade ate so early Mark wasn't sure it could technically be called lunch. At the request of several children, he wrote down the title and author of the book so that interested readers could finish the story on their own or with their parents. As he stood to go, Vicki ran to give him a hug.

"Thank you for coming to my class," she said.

"You're welcome, Bug."

"Wanna stay and have lunch with me?"

He wavered indecisively, having already missed a chunk of work today. "Another time?"

"Okay."

"But I'm going to do more stuff with your class, I promise. I'll stop by the front office and see if there's anything I can help with at night, when I'm not supposed to be at the store."

"You mean it?"

"Abso-posi-lutely."

True to his word, he spoke to Roberta Cree on his way out and discovered that there was a Woodside spirit night coming up at the local skating rink. He got the number for the person in charge so that he could call to volunteer his services as a chaperone.

Roberta skewered him with a pointed glance. "Was there something else you needed, Mr. Hathaway?"

"What? Oh. No. Sorry."

He realized with a start that he'd been lingering in the front office even though he already had what he needed and really should be getting back to work. Chastised, he turned to go. And assured himself that he had not been delaying in a subconscious and somewhat juvenile attempt to run into Shay Morgan.

"Principal Morgan, I may need your help."

Shay looked up from her notes for the Thursday

morning announcements with a smile. "That's what I'm here for, Mrs. Frost. Please, come in." She was glad for the opportunity to assist, to win over the faculty even if it was one member at a time. "What can I do for you?"

Mrs. Frost sighed. "With everything you must have on your schedule, I feel silly coming to you with something so small, but…"

"If it affects a student, nothing is too small for my time. Would you like to have a seat?"

"That's all right. I need to get back to my classroom before the kids start arriving, so I only have a minute." The teacher fidgeted with the reading glasses she wore on a gold chain around her neck. "I got an email last night from a parent. I know you've only been with us a few weeks, but I trust you're familiar with PTA vice president Carolyn Moon?"

Painfully so. "I am. Is Mrs. Moon unhappy about something?" Shay asked sympathetically.

Mrs. Frost nodded. "Mark Hathaway, another one of my parents, read to the class yesterday."

At the mention of Mark's name, a shiver of static electricity passed over Shay's body. Vicki's dad had amazing silvery eyes—and an even more amazing smile she sensed he didn't use enough. "Right. I encouraged him to get more involved and was pleased to note he was following through. Did…it not go well?"

"He was great! The kids loved him, so much that Lorelai Moon went to the media center during her afternoon free center and checked out the book he'd started. It was a chapter book, a bit above grade level, and we didn't have time to finish. Unfortunately, in one of the later chapters, the older brother in the story discusses with his younger brother that there's no Santa Claus.

Lorelai became very upset with this scene and the suggestion that all parents are big fat liars."

"Ergo Lorelai's mother is very upset." Shay suppressed a groan.

"Her reasoning was that he probably hadn't even read the book all the way through before, which made it an irresponsible selection for sharing with a roomful of six-year-olds and that he should have stuck to something more age appropriate." Mrs. Frost narrowed her eyes. They glimmered with momentary feistiness. "Of course, this is the same woman who encourages her daughter to strive for higher reading levels. Half the books Lorelai checks out are intended for third graders or above!"

The teacher drew a steadying breath. "I can send an email out to my class parents suggesting that future readers stick to picture books, simply because they're easier to finish in the time allotted. But Mrs. Moon is demanding that I speak to Mr. Hathaway about his 'inappropriate choice' to make sure nothing like this happens again. The last thing I want to do is discourage a parent who's just made his first foray into the classroom! However…"

"You feel like you need to mollify Carolyn," Shay deduced.

"Call me a big coward," Mrs. Frost said apologetically, "but I would hate to get caught between two of my parents. That could make some of our spring events awkward. I was hoping I could pass the buck."

"Of course. That's part of my job, handling the politics so that my teachers are free to focus on educating instead of toxic parents." After a beat, Shay added, "You do know I was speaking in generalities and not actually calling our PTA vice president toxic."

Mrs. Frost grinned. "Oh, I knew exactly what you meant."

"Glad we're on the same page," Shay said.

"I haven't responded to Mrs. Moon yet. Can I tell her that you've agreed to discuss the situation with Mr. Hathaway?"

"Actually, why don't you hold off on emailing her? I'll get in touch with her on your behalf, let her know that you dutifully passed on her concerns."

"Thank you." Mrs. Frost's shoulders sagged with relief. "I'm sure you'll handle the situation very diplomatically. And no doubt Mr. Hathaway will appreciate hearing from you instead of me. Rebuke probably doesn't sting as much when it's delivered by a pretty young blonde."

Shay's smile faltered. She knew that Mrs. Frost hadn't meant anything demeaning or disrespectful by her casual comment, but to a professional woman who occasionally struggled to get her colleagues, not to mention her parents, to take her seriously, it rankled. At a holiday-themed district fundraiser, the wife of one of the school board members had "congratulated" Shay on her appointment to Woodside. Knowing that the woman was reportedly bitter over her husband's numerous affairs hadn't made the moment less uncomfortable.

"Quite a coup for you, dear, becoming principal at your age. Why, you don't even have your doctorate." It wasn't a job requirement, but principals and even some vice principals holding PhDs was becoming more common in many districts. Then she'd flashed a smile that wasn't even in the same time zone as her eyes. "But the superintendent obviously sees your...other attributes."

"Is everything all right?" Mrs. Frost asked with a frown.

"Right as rain," Shay said, borrowing an old expression of her mother's. "You go ahead, see to your class, and I'll make sure I find time today to speak with Mrs. Moon and Mr. Hathaway." She thought about Carolyn Moon's perpetually pinched expression and then about Mark Hathaway, who had made her feel momentarily light-headed when he'd grinned down at her yesterday.

She added Geneva to her mental "will call" list. Today might require a little coconut-and-chocolate therapy.

"Up a Creek. Mark Hathaway speaking."

Shay smiled into the receiver. Mark's voice was a lovely contrast to the hostile man who'd just finished screaming at her about his daughter's grades. "Good afternoon, Mr. Hathaway. It's Principal Morgan."

"I've been meaning to call you," he said quickly. "When I told you yesterday that I wanted to discuss a volunteer opportunity, I wasn't just being flippant. I truly—"

She chuckled softly. "I believe you. I wasn't calling to nag."

"So, to what do I owe the pleasure? Don't tell me, Vicki's hacked into the school website and has posted my picture with the caption 'please marry this man.'"

Shay laughed outright this time. A few minutes' conversation with Mark was proving nearly as effective as one of Geneva's handmade dark chocolate bites rolled in shaved coconut and crushed macadamia pieces. "Nothing that serious. But I did have one minor thing I needed to mention. You know the book that you read to Vicki's class yesterday?"

"Yeah. She wanted us to finish it together last night, but we ran out of time before she had to go to bed."

"If you're reading it out loud to her, you might want to do some selective editing. We had a parent complaint that the story explains that there's not really a Santa Claus."

There was a long silence. "Oops."

"On the flip side, this is a public school, a melting pot of ages and cultural backgrounds. Occasionally kids in older grades will tell younger students that Santa doesn't exist, and some families don't observe the Santa tradition at all, so it's not as if this 'controversy' never arises." Shay stopped, bemused by her efforts to console him over the honest mistake. "Anyway, just as a general rule of thumb, you should probably stick to books for younger readers or make sure you're familiar with the content before you share them. Actually, the latter is probably the best practice since even different children's authors can vary wildly in what they deem appropriate."

"Of course."

"And I hope my calling in no way dissuades you from coming back. Mrs. Frost said you were a big hit with the kids."

"Just not with the parents," he said ruefully. "Which probably makes this a bad time to talk about further volunteer efforts."

"Not at all! What did you have in mind?" She was eager for him to try again—partly for his own benefit but also so she'd be secure in the knowledge that she hadn't run off a wonderful new volunteer.

"Well, I've already signed up for the skate night next week."

"Fantastic. When I had my own classroom, I always

went to our skate nights, but I haven't laced up a pair of roller skates in a few years. No laughing if you see me on Tuesday, okay?"

"Not to your face, anyway."

"Oh, and I suppose you're an expert," she scoffed.

"Sports and recreation guru, remember? My store sells in-line skates and I used to do beginner seminars in the empty lot behind us. Did you know you can burn 1,200 calories in about two and a half hours?"

Great. That was probably the approximate calorie count of one dark chocolate ball. With a sigh, she resolved to visit Geneva at her store less and in her workout room more.

"Anyway, the rink rents traditional roller skates, but they allow you to bring in your own in-line skates if you have them. I know where you could get a great deal on a pair if you're interested," he teased.

"So was the skate night what you wanted to discuss with me yesterday?" she asked.

"Uh, no." His previously joking tone became bashful. "Turns out, Vicki wanted to be a Campside Girl. She confirmed what you told me, about there not being enough leaders. So, I was wondering. I know they're the Campside Girls, but are men allowed to be troop leaders?"

Shay was thrown by his request. Being a troop leader would take a serious time investment, far more than a single classroom visit or an event like the Fitness Fair, which required a lot of preparation but had a definitive end date. "Okay, I have to ask," she said, recalling what he'd said during their first meeting but keeping her tone light, "you wouldn't try to revive our school's Campside

Girls chapter just to garner a few equipment sales at your store, right?"

"Not *just* to boost sales, no."

The smile in his voice reassured her that he hadn't taken offense. "I'll check into it for you. I bet you'd look smashing in the traditional Campside Girls uniform and butterfly beret."

Instead of retorting with a joke of his own, he replied solemnly, "I'd wear it in a heartbeat if it made my daughter's life better."

Shay blinked, touched by his earnest words. Mark and Vicki might not physically resemble each other but, recalling the little girl's hug on Monday, Shay realized that father and daughter had a lot in common. Currently topping the list was how much they both tugged at her heartstrings.

Chapter Six

"This isn't really what you guys do for fun in Braeden, is it?" Shay couldn't resist needling Geneva as they climbed out of her friend's two-door car, parallel parked across from town hall.

Geneva pocketed her keys, giving her a pointed look across the car's roof. "Oh, like you had such hot plans for your Thursday night before I invited you to tag along?"

Finalizing a state grant request for music education at Woodside probably didn't qualify as "hot."

"As a local small business owner," Geneva said, "it behooves me to network at these council meetings. And it behooves you, as a single woman new to town, to mingle. Have you met one guy since you moved here who wasn't a school kid enrolled in grades K through five?"

Mark Hathaway.

This wasn't a new thought—the man had been on Shay's mind all afternoon. First they'd had their phone conversation, which had been both charming and poignant. Then she'd called Carolyn Moon to let her know the situation was resolved; when the churlish woman seemed unwilling to drop her grudge, Shay had found herself defending Mark's innocent mistake.

Geneva stopped in her tracks, studying Shay intently beneath the streetlights. "Ohmigosh, have you met a man?"

"Lots of them," Shay prevaricated. "Fathers, a few male teachers, members of the school board."

"No one who isn't work-related?" Geneva pressed.

"Nope." And that was the God's honest truth.

"If you had, though, you'd tell me, right? As your closest friend here in Braeden, the person who could withhold coconut-macadamia bars from you?"

Shay snorted. "That sounds more like extortion than friendship. Could we please hurry it up inside? It's freezing out here."

Secretly, she was grateful for the stinging cold—it gave her an easy excuse for rosy cheeks. When they'd been kids, her brother Bastien had found it amusing to tease her until she blushed, which was impossible to hide with her fair coloring. But she wasn't a kid now; the fact that thinking about Mark could bring color to her face made her feel silly.

It was warm and cheerfully noisy inside. Although there wasn't a huge crowd, at least a couple of people dotted each row of seats. At the front of the room, chairs on the dais were still empty as council members worked the floor, shaking hands and greeting citizens by name.

But Shay was a little surprised to hear someone call *her* name.

"Principal Morgan?"

Even before she turned, she recognized the voice. And felt her cheeks warming again, darn it. "Mr. Hathaway.

Nice to see you." Boy, was it! Standing one row behind her, Mark was dressed more casually than on the previous occasions when he'd come from work. He wore a pair of faded jeans that fit as if he'd spent years breaking them in and a battered leather jacket over a charcoal V-neck that made his eyes even more intense. Shay wondered if anyone had ever suggested he dress like this to manage his store—he'd be able to sell the women of Braeden anything he wanted.

The only thing in the room as strong as Mark Hathaway's appeal was the power of Geneva's curiosity. Shay could feel her friend's questioning stare bore right through her. "Mr. Hathaway, this is my friend Geneva Daniels."

Mark smiled. "We've met once or twice. You run Book 'Em, right? My wife used to take our daughter, Vicki, in to the bookstore for story time. And as I recall, you sell a wicked cup of coffee."

"That's me." Geneva was all dimples as she nodded. "So is your daughter how you know Shay? Through the school, I mean?"

Mark's smile widened, his eyes crinkling as he exchanged amused glances with Shay. "Oh, yeah. Thanks to Vicki, I got called to the principal's office last week. Your friend here really knows how to lay down the law with parents."

"Hey," Shay protested with mock indignation. "It's not like I'm an ogre."

His gaze, still locked with hers, turned smoky. "Definitely not."

Moments like this must be how the cliché originated. Because for a brief second, Shay honestly did feel as if they were the only two in the room. She gave herself a mental shake. What was she, thirteen? The only way she could possibly be more trite was if their eyes had locked through the crowd, at a distance.

Nope, very little distance here, an irreverent corner of her mind noted happily. The only thing between them was a folding chair. On the other side of the metal, Mark stood close enough that she could breathe in the crisp, clean scent of soap and fainter smell of leather. When she realized she was on the verge of closing her eyes and inhaling deeply, she took a step backward. How could she ever expect parents and faculty to take her seriously if she swooned her way through a town council meeting?

"Ow," Geneva complained. "You mashed my toe."

"S-sorry," Shay said. "Maybe we should just take our seats. They'll probably be starting soon, don't you think?"

"We've got empty seats in our row," Mark said. "You could come sit with us."

"'Us?' You and your wife?" Geneva asked, making Shay wince.

"Mark's widowed," Shay said quickly, wanting to spare him the explanation.

"Oh. God, I'm so sorry."

Shay knew her friend was offering condolences both for the loss of his spouse and her question.

Mark inclined his head in gracious acceptance. "Actually I'm here with a buddy of mine. We were planning to grab some barbecue after the meeting, if you ladies would like to join us." He pointed across the room where an extremely tall man with broad shoulders stood in conversation with a council member in a suit and tie. "Cade Montgomery, carpenter and expert river guide."

Geneva's lips parted in a silent O, but she quickly regained her composure. "We'd *love* to have dinner with you."

The chairs were spaced very closely together, with little room left for maneuvering. To join the men in their row, Geneva and Shay first wound their way back to the center aisle. Shay took the opportunity to jab her friend in the shoulder.

"We couldn't have discussed the dinner idea first?" Shay demanded in a whisper.

"Oh, come on, did you *see* Cade Montgomery? I can't wait to see him up close! Besides, it looked like you and Mark had some chemistry of your own."

"He's a dad at the school," Shay said, "who may not be over his wife. And you know I'm not interested in dating anyone right now."

"Well, I might be! Do this for me, please? It won't kill you to have some yummy barbecue and an hour or so of pleasant conversation. Just don't do any flirting with Cade. Since you're not interested in men, I don't feel guilty about calling dibs."

Shay chuckled at her friend's phrasing. "He's a grown man, Gen, not the last slice of cheesecake."

Geneva grinned over her shoulder. "I was thinking more along the lines of beefcake."

There was a certain rugged appeal about Cade. His rich brown hair was a little shaggy, his features blunt, his forehead pronounced—the cumulative effect was of overwhelming masculinity. Objectively, Shay could appreciate the beauty in that. On the other hand, she was surprised her friend could be so taken by someone like Cade with Mark Hathaway in the room.

But in a moment of totally honest self-clarity, Shay

realized that if Geneva had fallen for Mark's charm...
It would have bothered me. She wasn't sure she would
have called her response jealousy—after all, she had no
claim on him—but the thought of him asking out her
best friend caused an unpleasant rising sensation in her
stomach. Like a time she'd eaten bad eggs.

The two women reached Mark at about the same time
as Cade did.

With a raised eyebrow, the carpenter/river guide
smiled at Mark. "In the few minutes I was gone, you
found two beautiful women and convinced them to sit
with us? Outstanding."

Grinning, Geneva thrust out her hand. "Geneva Daniels. I own a bookstore on the square."

"Cade Montgomery." He shook her hand. "And if I'd
known you were in the bookstore, I would have taken
up reading."

Mark snorted. "Please. One entire wall of this guy's
living room is built-in bookshelves."

"And I haven't seen you in my store? I'm heartbro-
ken," Geneva said.

"I admit, I've fallen into the habit of buying books
online, but I'm feeling a sudden civic duty to support
local businesses. After the council meeting, maybe
you can tell me all about what's new on the shelves."
Cade switched his gaze to Shay. "We haven't met yet,
either."

Mark took over the introductions. "This is Shay
Morgan."

"The new principal at Woodside," she added.

"*You're* Ridenour's replacement?" Cade's eyes
widened.

On the dais, the town mayor banged a gavel, inviting

everyone to take their seats so that the meeting could begin. Geneva positioned herself on Cade's right. The two men sat in the middle, with Shay on the far left. Cade muttered something to Mark. Though Shay couldn't make out the words, she noticed that Cade poked his friend in the ribs and that Mark tried unsuccessfully to smother a laugh.

Town meetings in Braeden were conducted by the mayor, four other council members, a town manager and the town clerk, who kicked things off by reading the minutes of last month's session. Official business consisted of amending several local ordinances, naming the contractor who had been chosen for a historic building restoration and finalizing plans for the upcoming, Valentine-themed "Have a Heart" blood drive. Then the council opened the meeting for comments, questions and concerns from the floor.

Cade Montgomery was recognized and got to his feet. "We should take this opportunity to welcome Principal Shay Morgan, who's new to Braeden and attending her first town meeting. I hear she's doing a fantastic job over at Woodside watching out for the town's little ones and making sure they get the best education possible."

Shay was startled by this unexpected acknowledgment and the applause that followed.

"You should stand up and wave," Mark whispered.

She did, even though it made her feel as if she were on the back of some parade float. From her standing position, she couldn't miss the woman three rows up who turned—Carolyn Moon. *Oh, joy.* The woman's gaze dropped from Shay to Mark, seated next to her, and she narrowed her green eyes. Shay plopped down in her seat.

As she did so, her body brushed Mark's. Awareness shot through her like an arrow.

She swallowed, keeping her voice low as the next speaker began her remarks. "Sorry. These, uh, chairs are awfully close together. None of the rows except the front ones are full—maybe they should space things out better next time, give people more elbow room."

"Oh, I don't know." Mark kept his gaze straight ahead, but his grin was just as disarming in profile. "The current seating arrangement's not without its perks."

Like being scant centimeters from the hottest guy she'd met since college? No argument there.

Shay blinked, reminding herself she was an adult and a consummate professional. Her mind was only wandering to inappropriate places because the council meeting was a bit dry. *Any* woman would find watching the curve of Mark's mouth as he smiled more stimulating than listening to the pros and cons of outlawing decorative novelty mailboxes.

The next fifteen minutes dragged on while various citizens stood to say their piece. But after a lady in the back stood to thank the council for its diligence in quickly responding to a massive pothole on Juniper Street, Mark raised his hand to be recognized. Shay straightened in her seat. The meeting had just become interesting.

"As some of you know, I'm Mark Hathaway, manager of Up A Creek and a local father. I wanted to take a few minutes of your time tonight to talk about the Douglas Lodge that was closed down. If you're unfamiliar with its history, it was originally built as a polling place for people who lived out in the sticks." He said it with affection, clearly proud to live on the less-polished outskirts of urbanization. "Later it passed into private ownership and was refurbished, serving as the main office for the nearby campsite. But in the past few years, it's been sitting derelict. I think we're overlooking a great opportunity for our town. The hiking and fishing possibilities near the lodge are as plentiful as they've ever been, and most of the surrounding park area is government owned. If the town took responsibility for the lodge itself, we could reopen camping in the area and encourage people from neighboring counties to come admire the beauty of what we have here in Braeden."

In the row in front of them, a man snickered and whispered to his companion, "'If you build it, they will come'?"

She slugged him in the arm. "Shut up, Harry. I happen to love that movie."

Mark ignored the byplay. "Plus, reopening the lodge provides us another opportunity to spend time with our own families, fostering an appreciation of nature."

"Which all sounds great," the mayor agreed. "As long as someone can pay to reopen the place, fix it up and pay whatever staff is needed."

"I understand that, sir. But I believe it's worth looking into and that, if marketed properly, the lodge could become a solid source of town revenue. Only a small portion of it is needed for office space. The rest could be rented out for events—banquets, corporate retreats or family reunions. Or the interior could be used for displays to form a small nature museum. Charge three-dollar admission for tours. For what it costs to buy our kids a popcorn at the movies, a parent could spend an hour helping them learn about our environment and wildlife, then enjoy some exercise in the fresh air."

"Says the man who owns a store that sells hiking and fishing accessories." Carolyn Moon swiveled in her chair, making sure that everyone in the back could hear her sniff in disdain.

"Mrs. Moon, you have not been recognized to speak," the town clerk reminded her, staring pointedly over the top of her horn-rimmed spectacles.

Mayor Green thanked the clerk, then turned back to Mark. "You've given this a lot of thought, Mr. Hathaway."

"Of course, sir. To stand here unprepared and ramble whatever came into my head would be a waste of the council's time."

The mayor encouraged Mark to make an appointment with the town planner to present his ideas and also encouraged the rest of the people attending the meeting to consider the matter so that voters' opinions could be heard in the future.

As the next person stood to speak, Shay leaned closer to whisper, "You did great. As soon as they open that nature museum, I'm putting a call in about school field trips."

With a smile, Mark reached over to squeeze her hand. She suspected it was meant to be a quick, wordless gesture of gratitude for her support. But his touch also turned out to be a quick way to short-circuit her brain and set her hormones buzzing. She didn't hear another word clearly for the rest of the meeting.

UNLIKE THE COUNCIL MEETING, which adhered to a formal structure and often turned dull for periodic stretches, their late dinner around a circular table at the barbecue house was fun, messy and verbally chaotic.

Shay was used to conversations with Geneva where the two of them were practically talking over top of each other, but it was even more frenetic with Cade interjecting outrageous comments and Mark playfully mocking them all. He teased his friend about his "he-man persona" and questioned aloud how Geneva and Shay ever managed to eat anything when they never stopped chatting. But it was patently obvious that he didn't mean the gibe because he laughed as loud as anyone at Geneva's irreverent jokes and, whenever conversation slowed for a nanosecond, asked Shay questions about herself, her job and how she liked living in Braeden.

Right at the moment, life in Braeden seemed pretty darn perfect.

In fact, if Mark hadn't noticed the time on the clock hanging opposite their table, Shay would have been content to sit there all night, swapping anecdotes and dragging fries through a tangy puddle of barbecue sauce, with no thought to how early she had to be up for work in the morning.

Mark frowned. "I hate to break up the party, but my sister-in-law is not a late-night person. I should get back so that Dee can go home and go to bed."

"The waitress just brought me another round," Cade said, tapping the side of his full pilsner glass. "And I really want to hear the rest of Gen's story about how she handled this nut-job customer. Geneva, would you mind swapping passengers with Mark? Maybe he could take Shay home, and you could drop me off later."

Geneva turned beseeching eyes to Shay. "You'd be okay with that, right?"

Shay sighed inwardly. A line had been crossed tonight—for the first time, they hadn't been "Principal

Morgan" and "Mr. Hathaway." They'd been Shay and Mark, laughing over a couple of beers, perilously close to flirting, but with four of them at the table, there'd been no real threat of intimacy. She wasn't sure leaving with him was the best idea ever. It was too easy to imagine other lines that could be crossed.

But just because dating was not her current priority and she doubted Mark was even emotionally ready to date...well, those weren't good reasons to sabotage Geneva's love life.

So she capitulated with a wan smile. "It's okay with me if it's okay with Mark."

"Great! You guys go ahead," Cade suggested before Mark could offer an opinion one way or another. "I'll get the check and we can settle up later."

"Wait, I have cash here." Shay dug into her purse, but both men were shaking their heads.

"Dinner's on us," Mark objected. "We invited you."

"Consider it a welcome to Braeden. And you," Cade told Geneva, "consider it an apology for my not frequenting your store in the past. I can assure you, that will be remedied."

She giggled, waggling her fingers in Shay's direction and not even looking up when Shay and Mark left the table.

"Thanks for the ride," Shay said as they stepped outside. A light drizzling rain had started while they ate, just enough to dampen the asphalt. The parking lot shone a slick silver.

"No problem. I wouldn't have gone straight home anyway since I had with Cade me." He paused, looking uncertain in the shadows. "You don't mind, do you—my taking you home? There was a moment inside where it seemed like you might not be comfortable with the idea."

She jammed her hands into the pockets of her jacket, wondering what to say. Although she didn't consider herself shy in general, she couldn't possibly tell him that she was attracted to him, which she found awkward, and that being alone with him only magnified the awkwardness. *Not to mention the attraction.* "I suppose I'm being hypersensitive. I'm the principal at your child's school, which is a fairly public position that invites a lot of scrutiny from parents and concerned community members. And you've had your own share of scrutiny since…"

He laughed softly, the sound like a warm breeze across the nape of her neck. "Since my daughter sent out a mass-mailing informing people that her dad couldn't get a date?"

"That is sort of where I was going, yeah." She bit her lip, worried she'd just embarrassed him and wishing she'd kept her mouth shut. "You know, it's really kind of a pretty night. Maybe I'll just walk."

They both grinned at each other. In addition to being cold, the raindrops were growing steadily heavier.

"As a dues-paying PTA member, I'm obligated to make sure the school principal doesn't get pneumonia on my watch." He opened the car door for her. "Hop in."

"You certainly seem to take your myriad duties seriously," she said, once they were both buckled into their seats and she'd told him the name of her subdivision. "Chauffeuring principals, being a father, running your store."

"Not actually mine," he clarified. "Carolyn was wrong about that."

There's a shock. In Shay's opinion, Carolyn was wrong about a great many things.

"I manage the Braeden location, but it's owned by a businessman who lives out of state." In the dark, it was hard to make out Mark's expression, but the tension in his voice was unmistakable. "He's thinking of shutting us down, actually. But I'd appreciate if we could keep that piece of information between us."

Shay's heart squeezed painfully. No wonder he'd been so cranky at their first meeting—facing possible unemployment would be difficult for anyone, much less a single father. "What would you do if the store closed?"

Mark was silent for so long that she regretted asking the question, afraid she'd upset him. But then he answered, "It won't happen. I won't let it. Carolyn was right about one thing. I do have ulterior motives for wanting to see outdoor recreation increase in the area."

"Hey, stimulating the local economy is ultimately good for all of us. But…even if they do reopen that lodge you were talking about, that's bound to take months, right? How much time do you have?"

"Not enough."

As determined as he was to keep the store up and running, on Monday morning, Mark wished he didn't have this job. Being in charge meant that you often had to be the bearer of bad news.

"Thank you both for coming in," he told Roddy and Keesha. The three of them were seated in the break room, where Mark had just poured them all coffee. He'd scheduled this meeting for what was typically a slow part of the day, asking Dee to watch the store for a little while. She could handle simple transactions but would come back to get one of them if anything complicated arose.

"Anything you need, boss," Roddy replied easily.

Keesha, however, squirmed in her seat, looking apprehensive. Mark wondered if she had a sixth sense about what he was planning to tell them.

Since stalling wouldn't make this any easier, he jumped right in with, "I'll talk to Ed and Joan later, but since they're part-time, it won't affect them as much. You both know that the store hasn't been doing as well in the past year and a half. The fact of the matter is that Coleridge is considering closing us down this spring if I can't improve our profit margin. I promise you both, I'm doing everything I can think of to make that happen— like the upcoming Valentine sale. And I welcome any ideas you have. In the meantime, I'm afraid I have to cut some costs. You both do a wonderful job and Lord knows, you deserve raises but—"

"You're letting one of us go?" Roddy interrupted, his face grim.

"No," Mark promised. *At least not yet.* He prayed it wouldn't come to that. While Vicki was his primary motivation for saving the store, there were other people he cared about who would also be affected. "But I need to cut your hours and possibly your pay. I don't want either of you to lose your benefits, so we'll be scaling back to meet the minimum requirement for 'full-time.'" He'd reduce his hours if it would help, but his salary was annual, not hourly.

"Mark, let me just stop you there." Surprisingly,

Keesha was smiling. "I can make this all a whole lot easier. I quit."

He blinked, startled by the announcement. "Keesha—"

"It's not because I'm angry. I respect you and know you're trying to do right by us. But I was struggling with a hard choice. Like you said, we all knew the store hasn't been doing too well. I've done a lot of volunteer work for my church over the years, including their newsletter, and our receptionist just retired. They offered me her job, but I wasn't sure what to tell them. It would have meant a pay cut and you've been good to me, so I felt loyal to the store. But now…"

Mark's lungs expanded fully for the first time all day. Ever since he woke up that morning, he'd felt like he had a brick of guilt sitting on his chest that made it impossible to breathe. "We'll miss you, of course, but it sounds as if this will be the right move for you."

Roddy patted his coworker on the arm, quietly congratulating her on the new job. Then he asked Mark, "So are my hours still going down?"

Mark shook his head. "Nope, guess not."

Keesha flashed them an impish grin. "Are you kidding? You two will have to pick up my slack."

She was right. Down one full-time employee, Mark would probably need to work more. Because he didn't get paid hourly, there was no overtime pay, which would be a concern with Roddy.

Mark frowned. Shay had emailed him on Friday that she would have an answer soon on whether he could head up a Campside troop. Although it wasn't yet definite, she'd been optimistic that he'd get approval. Mark had happily anticipated giving good news to his daughter this week. Now he was torn, not sure if he wanted to be made a troop leader or rejected, leaving him more time and mental energy to deal with his job.

But then he recalled Vicki's animated expression when she'd been talking over the weekend about the "cute butterfly hats" Campside Girls got to wear and how many times she'd said "thank you, Daddy!" ever since he offered to be a leader. And suddenly he didn't feel conflicted anymore. He would find a way to do both. He just had to commit to his goals—be the best dad possible to Vicki, keep the store alive—and stay focused on achieving them.

Chapter Seven

Multicolored lights flashed above a slick circular floor, and some song that was currently popular with kids blared through the speakers. Given the high-pitched voice, Mark had assumed they were listening to a female singer. But when he asked who "she" was, the third-grade sister of Vicki's best friend laughingly informed him it was Jace-somebody, a preteen singing sensation who was *so cute*.

Mark flashed the girl a smile. "I'll take your word for it."

When he and Vicki had walked through the turn-stile and into the roller rink, her friend Tessa Wilkes had spotted them immediately, waving and screaming hellos. The girls had been in class together for kinder-garten and again this year; their first order of business at any event was to find each other. Tessa and her big sister, Heather, were here with their mom, Charlotte, a woman who barely topped five feet. The girls, however had inherited their height from their lanky father, and would clearly dwarf their mom in the next few years. Mr. Wilkes was a night manager at a factory outside town, often available to visit his girls for lunch and pick them up after school, but frequently missing evening activities like tonight's.

Mark had been embarrassed at the winter carnival when he and Charlotte realized that, in Mr. Wilkes's absence, Vicki was pretending that her dad was married to Tessa's mom and that they were a family. Charlotte had been sympathetic and maybe even a little amused; her daughters, understandably protective of their parents' marriage, had not been.

"I know you have a husband," Vicki had told Charlotte, "but I like to use my 'magination and have a mommy, too."

With that incident in mind—and thinking it would be good for him and Charlotte to keep unmistakable space between them—Mark finished lacing up his daughter's skates and turned her over to Mrs. Wilkes for safekeeping. She assured him that Vicki would be fine with them for however long he needed. Mark was scheduled to work a shift at the school's sign-in booth, helping to keep track of how much business Woodside had created for the rink tonight and handing out raffle tickets for the door prizes that would be awarded later in the evening.

The Woodside table, decorated in the school's yellow and green colors and a stuffed frog to represent their mascot, sat just inside the main entrance, near the admissions booth everyone had to use. An auburn-haired woman was already seated there, and Mark smiled in greeting as he took the chair next to her.

"Ah, they corralled a dad into helping tonight." The redhead smiled at him. "I'm Anita Shepherd, mother of third-grade twins."

"Mark Hathaway. I have a six-year-old daughter in Mrs. Frost's class."

"You don't have any older children?" The woman paused, her expression perplexed. "Because your name sounds so… *Oh*. I know why your name is familiar. I believe we got an email from your daughter," she explained, although he'd already deduced that for himself.

"You and lots of other people," he said, trying to sound good-natured instead of aggrieved. "Kids say the darnedest things. Or type the darnedest things, in this case."

Anita laughed. "If I may be so bold, Mark, I have a younger sister near Asheville who's had trouble meeting the right guy. And—"

"Oh, look, a Woodside family," he said brightly. His voice was a bit too loud when he called out to the foursome who had just come through the turnstile. "Good evening! Welcome to Woodside's spirit night. If I could get you to come sign in, we have a few goodies for you." He gave a pencil to the boy in the group, a sticker to the girl and raffle tickets to the parents.

A steady stream of people flowed through the doors, including Dee and Frank with Bobby—who parted ways with them as soon as they'd paid his admittance, barely acknowledging that he knew the people who'd given him life. Frank headed for the concessions stand, saying that he hadn't had a chance to eat anything between getting home from work and leaving for the rink.

Dee remained at the table, teasing her brother-in-law with a proud smile. "Look at you being all helpful! Of course, now that you've proven that you're reliable, I'll be calling on you to help with next year's book fair."

Mark's smile faded. *If we're still here by then.*

Dee didn't notice his expression. She was busy scanning the dim interior. The lights of the arcade and above the skating floor were more about flash and dramatic effect than actually keeping it bright enough to see inside. Mark had brought Jessica here—technically, his mom had dropped them off—when he was fifteen and Jess had giggled that the "mood lighting" was very romantic.

"Where's your little one?" Dee asked, having failed to locate Vicki.

"With Charlotte Wilkes and her girls." Mark checked his watch. "Although I'm almost done with my shift here, so I'll go reclaim her soon."

"Before you go," Anita Shepherd interrupted, "you've got to see this." While he'd been chatting with Dee, Anita had been digging through her purse. "Here, I knew this was in my wallet somewhere."

She slapped a picture into his palm of a green-eyed woman with lots of freckles and pretty features.

"My sister, Layla. Lovely, isn't she?" Anita glanced up to enlist Dee's help. "Don't you think they'd make a cute couple?"

Dee's lips twitched, her eyes glinting with amusement as she took in Mark's discomfort. "Um, I'd better go find my husband and remind him he's not eighteen anymore before he wolfs down a jalapeno dog and a jumbo slice of pizza and is up all night with heartburn."

Mark passed the picture back to its owner. "Your sister is very pretty and I wish her all the best finding the right guy. But to be honest, I'm not really looking for a relationship right now."

"Does your daughter know that?" the woman asked with a smile.

"Well, I've told her, but I'm not sure it's sinking in."

Two more mothers approached the table, ready to take over the next shift so that Anita and Mark could enjoy the evening with their own families. Mark pushed back his chair. As he was standing, he saw Shay come through the turnstile. She looked beautiful in a red-and-gray tunic over darker gray leggings, her blond hair pulled back in some sort of elegant twist that seemed far too classy for her surroundings. But she also looked tired, as if she'd had a long day.

Then she spotted him and a wide smile brightened her face. Watching the transformation in her demeanor, he was flattered but a little taken aback. Was it possible that simply seeing him was enough to improve her mood?

He considered it from the other angle. Hadn't his mood lifted when he saw Shay enter the building? *Yes.* He ran a hand through his hair, not entirely comfortable with his realization. He'd only known the principal for a couple of weeks, yet there was no denying that she had a palpable effect on him.

Shay approached the volunteer table. Although she made eye contact with Mark, she looked away and spoke to the other parents first, greeting each mother by name before coming back to him. "And Mr. Hathaway, always nice to see you. In fact, I have some news I'm supposed to pass along to you. Do you have a minute?"

He nodded. "I was all finished here."

They decided to find a table in the concession area, which was farthest from the blaring speakers above the skate floor.

Mark had been a married man long enough to learn that you never tell a woman she "looks tired." Instead, as he slid onto a bench seat across from Shay, he simply said, "You seemed pensive when you came in. Tough day, or were you just lost in thought?"

She cocked her head, looking surprised by the question. "A little of both, I guess." She rolled her shoulders. "I love my job—I'm doing exactly what I want with my life and not everyone gets to say that. But it's not always easy."

"Well, of course not. After all, you have to deal with parents on a daily basis." He smiled. "We're pretty obnoxious."

"Not all of you," she said softly. "And it's not just the parents who bring me down—we have some truly wonderful families at Woodside. But the administrative red tape can be frustrating and the budget is crazy-making. Our school district, like a lot of others, isn't in great financial shape. It pains me to think of good teachers losing their jobs or students losing out on programs that are really beneficial because there's not enough funding."

"I can only imagine," Mark commiserated with a shake of his head. "On a much smaller scale, I had to deal with some of that today. I had to bring in my two full-time employees, the ones who've been with me the longest, and tell them that we were looking at pay cuts. I hated to do it. Luckily, one of them quit."

Shay's brows drew together. "Luckily?"

He chuckled. "She's been offered another job and was feeling guilty about maybe taking it. I don't think she feels guilty about it anymore."

"Glad it worked out for the best. How's everything else going at the store?" she asked. "Did you get an appointment with the town planner?"

He nodded. "But not until next week—his schedule

was pretty full. On Friday, I'm driving out to Hawk Summit to meet with the director of operations about cross-promotional sales and events. And we're doing a weeklong Valentine's sale at the store that starts Saturday, encouraging people to show their love for others by helping each other stay healthy. It's a buy-one-get-one-free event, good for anything in the store under a hundred dollars. People can purchase his and hers tennis rackets or bike helmets, that kind of thing. Or even a Valentine's gift for a friend or family member."

Shay snapped her fingers. "Perfect. Geneva and I have been talking about each getting an exercise ball for our workout regimen." She groaned.

"Problem?"

"No, no problem. More like a realization." She glanced down at the table, a mild blush staining her cheeks. Her tone was sheepish. "I'm a lousy sister. It's just…it occurred to me that my big brother, Bastien, will spend his Valentine's Day proposing to his girlfriend while I will be marking the holiday by giving exercise equipment to my friend. Not that I'm looking for romance," she added so quickly that, under other circumstances, Mark might have been insulted. "But I guess no matter how old you are, it's impossible to completely outgrow sibling rivalry. Do you have any sisters or brothers?"

"Only child. But Dee is exactly what I imagine an older sister would be like. Caring, fiercely loyal, bossy, opinionated, no qualms about mocking me," he said with a grin. "Vicki and I are lucky that Dee and Frank adopted us after we lost Jess."

"Speaking of Vicki!" Shay shook her head as if trying

to clear it. "Sorry. I came over here to deliver some good news, then got so caught up in talking to you…"

"Time flies, doesn't it?" He'd been shocked at how quickly their dinner had gone by at the barbecue house, without a single awkward pause to mar the evening. He'd attributed most of that to Geneva and Cade being there. The bookstore owner seemed naturally gregarious and Cade was never at a loss with women. But now, even when it was just the two of them, Mark still fell into a comfortable rhythm talking to Shay. He supposed it was easy because he legitimately wanted to hear all about her day, learn about her and what she was thinking, wanted to make her laugh when she was troubled and wanted to enjoy laughing with her. When was the last time he'd experienced that with a woman?

His insides twisted. He knew *exactly* when he'd last experienced that, with whom he'd last shared such a connection.

"I've heard back from the regional Campside Girls leader and also talked to our PTA president," Shay said. "You're officially approved to be a troop leader! There are a few conditions, but they're standard operating procedure for the protection of the kids, nothing personal. Regular meetings can be held in the Woodside cafeteria, but for any outside excursions, you must have at least one female volunteer with you. The good news is, it doesn't have to be the same person every time. I think you'll have an easier job finding people to commit to one event or camping trip than we did finding a permanent leader."

Permanent? Signing up as troop leader suddenly sounded like a life sentence, but he refused to second-guess his decision when he knew how happy this would make his daughter. "I can't wait to tell Vicki." He got to his feet, imagining her smile. "She's gonna be over the moon!"

Shay looked delighted for both of them. "I think this is really going to be good for both of you. And, on a selfish note," she said as she rose, "fabulous for the girls at Woodside who otherwise wouldn't have been able to participate. I assume that you'll want to get started as soon as possible?"

Troop activities, Mark knew from his research over the past week, followed the calendar year rather than the school year. There should have been an orientation and sign up in November, before all the holidays, but actual meetings wouldn't have started until January. With February just starting, they weren't that far behind other schools—yet.

"You bet." He experienced a twinge, wondering if it was irresponsible for him to take on a project that lasted until December when he and Vicki might have to leave over the summer. *Don't think like that.* Thousands of people believed in the power of positive thinking—why couldn't he be one of them?

Then again, positive thinking had failed him in the past.

Instead of relying on hope, he analyzed the situation realistically. Surely in the history of Campside Girls, a troop leader had found out she had to relocate. Either another parent would step up to fill Mark's shoes—maybe someone would be more willing to finish out a partial term with a troop that had already formed than start up a completely new year—or the troop would disband. Which would be unfortunate, but the girls would be no worse off than they already were. In the meantime,

Mark would throw himself into making sure they got the most out of the experience while he was in charge.

"Mark?" Shay eyed him warily. "You're not regretting taking this on, are you? I thought you'd be happier."

"No, I'm thrilled. Just...wanna do my best, you know?"

She smiled. "I know. That's how I feel every single time I pull into the school parking lot. Anyway, if you're ready to get started, I'll have a memo typed up and sent home with all our first- and second-grade girls this week! Good luck."

"I'm sure I'll need it," he admitted.

"Just do me one favor..." Darting a glance around as if checking for eavesdroppers, she suddenly stepped close to him.

So close that he could feel the warmth of her curves and breathe in the unexpected, summery raspberry scent of her skin—body wash, maybe? A split-second image of Shay in the shower seared his brain. He hardened at the thought, so caught off guard by the intensity of his reaction that he nearly stumbled.

"Mark?" As she had only moments ago, she said his name. But it was softer this time, breathier. And there was no questioning wariness in her expression. Was it his imagination or did her aquamarine eyes mirror—

"Well." In comparison to Carolyn Moon's smug voice, fingernails on a chalkboard were a symphony. "Don't the two of *you* look cozy?"

Mark swung his head to the side, ashamed. Vicki could have walked up with her aunt, uncle, cousin and the entire Wilkes family and he wouldn't have noticed. He'd been too busy lusting after her principal. At an elementary school function.

"Carolyn." There was a waver to Shay's voice and Mark knew instinctively that her reflex had been to jerk back, away from him, but she stood frozen in place. As if backing up would have made her look guilty of a crime she hadn't committed. *Yet*. "Good news. I was just telling Mr. Hathaway here that he's been approved as a Campside Girls leader, so thanks to his willingness to volunteer, it's going to be possible for our school to host a troop! Isn't that wonderful? Maybe your Lorelai will be interested in joining."

Mark could have kicked her on the shin for that—like he needed any more time spent in Carolyn Moon's proximity—but he needn't have worried. Carolyn crinkled her nose as if offended by Shay's comment.

"Lorelai is quite busy with her other activities— ballet, piano, choir. Even with a natural gift, it requires hours of practice for a little girl to become as talented as she is."

"So it does." Shay's smile was so big and bright that Mark was surprised Carolyn wasn't blinking against its glare. "Was there something you needed me for?"

"N-no. I just… Well, I just stopped by to say hello. As any polite person would."

Bull. She'd stopped by to pass judgment, to make Shay—or both of them—uncomfortable. Mark recalled Shay's words outside the barbecue house. She'd said that being the principal was "a fairly public position that invites a lot of scrutiny." Now he had firsthand experience with exactly what she meant. If she was ever seen kissing a parent from the school—not that she had!—people would discuss it. If she, heaven forbid, let her hair down some weekend and performed a wild musical number at Tasting Notes, a local restaurant that offered Braeden's only karaoke, everyone would know by Monday morning. Mark couldn't really conceive of that kind of pressure, being a fair target for gossip because of the job you held. He'd always been more of a team player than soloist, used to being part of the local scenery. The only time he'd ever felt painfully visible was in the weeks after Jess's death, when well-meaning people he barely even knew had accosted him on the street to offer their condolences.

"Ah. Hello, then." The way Shay said it, the word was clearly meant as a goodbye.

Carolyn's lips pursed. "I'll just let the two of you get back to your...discussion. Good night."

"Have a nice evening," Mark managed. *Just do it far away from Shay.*

As the woman exited the semienclosed concession area, Shay hissed out a breath.

"I am the principal," she muttered, "and I appreciate all of the parents who give their time and efforts and make Woodside the wonderful school that it is."

He grinned. "But?"

"If I was going to take an extreme dislike to one of them..."

She stood there looking so adorably exasperated that he was tempted for a second to drop a kiss on her forehead. The idea of that tender gesture was as jarring, in a different way, as the lust he'd experienced earlier.

"So." He swallowed. "You were going to stay something? Before we were interrupted."

"Right. I was going to ask you a favor regarding your new role with the Campside Girls. Well, actually, more like give you a friendly piece of advice." With a wickedly teasing grin, she lowered her voice to a whisper. "Try to avoid telling them there's no Easter Bunny, would you?"

"CAN I HAVE A DRINK, DADDY?"

Mark studied his daughter's face, bright with excitement and flushed with exertion from her many laps around the skating floor. God, he loved that little face, the eyes that were so much like her mom's, the smile that hadn't changed since Vicki was a chubby baby who'd wrenched his heart with the pure sweetness of her first laugh.

"Yeah, beverages sound like a good idea." He was thirsty himself after more skating than he'd done in years. "You having fun tonight?"

"The mostest!" she declared as they exited the skate floor. He was proud of how well she was doing. Even though she skated better than a lot of her friends, she'd still fallen a couple of times tonight—but she hadn't cried. In fact, the smile hadn't left her face since the moment he'd told her that he was the new Campside Girls leader. Dee had even become teary-eyed when she'd heard the news.

"It's a good thing you're doing," she'd told him as Vicki had rushed shrieking with joy to Tessa, asking if the little girl wanted to join the troop and if the Wilkeses knew if Valerie—another Campside hopeful—was still here. In a voice so low her words were barely audible over the cover of "Kung Fu Fighting" that was blasting, Dee admitted, "I really worried about the two you for a while. I mean, that comes with the territory, worrying about loved ones, but I think… You guys are going to be all right, no matter what happens. Jess would be proud of you."

The reminder of his late wife hadn't upset him as it once would have. He'd merely nodded, accepting the comment as the praise Dee had intended, choosing to believe that it was true.

"So what do you want to drink, Bug? A lemonade or—"

His daughter cut him off with a squeal. "Principal Morgan!" She skated toward the blonde so quickly—and without total mastery of stopping—that Shay wobbled a bit under the onslaught. If she'd been wearing skates herself, she probably would have fallen.

At the sight of Shay hugging his daughter, emotion welled in Mark, so powerful that he looked away.

"Did you hear? I get to be a Campside Girl!"

"I know. Isn't that wonderful of your dad to help you and all the other little girls?" Shay asked.

Vicki nodded enthusiastically, flailing her arms a bit as she tried to step away. Moving backward wasn't nearly as easy as forward. Mark gave his daughter a hand, supporting her so she didn't stumble. He glanced down at Shay's black suede demiboots.

"No skates? Come on, Principal Morgan, where's your sense of adventure?" he chided. "I did promise not to laugh at your attempts."

She arched an eyebrow. "As I recall, you qualified that you wouldn't laugh *to my face*. No, I did mean to get on the floor tonight, but I've been talking to parents and teachers and I guess time just got away from me."

"You could still do it," Vicki said. "I'll go with you if you want a friend."

Shay looked as if she was considering the little girl's offer. "Where were the two of you headed?"

"To get drinks," Mark said, "and then to say goodbye to Dee and her family. She mentioned getting home because Bobby wanted to do just a bit more studying for his science exam."

Shay absently bit her lower lip while she thought it over. "I suppose I could rent skates while you two got your refreshments."

"Yay!"

Even though Mark didn't vocally echo his daughter's sentiment, he felt pretty much the same way.

True to her word, the principal got a pair of roller skates—although Mark noticed that she got waylaid several times on her way to the skate counter. Even as he said good-night to the Riggs family, he found his gaze straying to wherever Shay was. Watching the way she smiled, the way she stilled and really seemed to listen to whomever was speaking. She was kind and funny, but she also had a sharp wit and, as he knew from their first meeting, wasn't afraid to speak her mind if she thought it was best for one of her students. While he knew she was fully aware of being scrutinized and hoped to garner strong parental support so that she could remain Woodside's principal, she hadn't backed down earlier when Carolyn Moon attempted to corner them.

All in all, Shay Morgan was a hell of a woman. The more he got to know her, the more he found to admire in her. Including, he discovered, her courage in going out onto the skate floor because the woman was seriously out of practice.

Even Vicki looked concerned, her feathery red-gold eyebrows drawn together. "We can skate closer to the rail if you want to hang on."

Shay laughed. "That's all right, sweetie. I used to be good at this—I just need a little practice to remember how it's done." Under her breath, she muttered, "Besides, the rail doesn't go all the way around." It was segmented into three short, intermittent lengths, mostly intended to help people as they entered and exited the rink.

They'd only executed a few laps when the guy working the DJ booth announced in the requisite low, cheesy baritone they must teach in some skating DJ class somewhere, "All right, this next song is for couples only. So come on, you lovebirds, out on the floor. Couples only."

With Vicki in the middle, the three of them skated toward the nearest off-ramp. The lights dimmed except for some sparkles thrown out on the floor by the disco ball and the opening notes of an '80s ballad played through the speakers. The moment was so unapologetically kitschy that Mark couldn't stifle his amusement. He met Shay's gaze over top of Vicki's head, and within seconds, the two of them were both cracking up.

"What?" Vicki glanced up, first confused and then glaring because no one had filled her in on the joke. "What's so funny?"

They all sat down on one of the long carpeted benches where people could rest or lace up their skates. Vicki snuggled into his side, obviously getting tired, and Shay smiled at him. Mark knew that, to some of the preteen boys rolling by with their girlfriends, holding hands while listening to a soulful song about roses and thorns probably seemed like the height of romance. But frankly, Mark thought he'd found an even better deal, sitting on the sidelines with a tired first grader and her pretty school principal.

Halfway through the guitar solo, Mark heard a girl ask, "Mr. Hathaway?" Heather Wilkes, Tessa's older sister, regarded him shyly. "Can you do me a favor?"

"I'll try. What do you need?"

"That's my friend, who's never been skating before." Heather pointed to where another girl, very petite next to Heather but probably about the same age, waved half-heartedly. "I've tried to get her on the floor all night, but she keeps chickening out, saying she wanted to wait until more people went home so no one would see if she fell. Only now, the whole thing's almost over."

Pausing, Heather rolled her eyes to show how she felt about her friend's procrastination. "She promised me she'll do the next song if an adult will go with us, but Mom's already turned in her skates. Will you go out on the floor with us?"

"Sure thing." It was the least he could do, considering how Charlotte Wilkes had kept an eye on Vicki for the first half of the evening. The rock ballad faded, giving way to a peppier song from a recent *American Idol* winner. Mark stood, asking his daughter and Shay, "Are you guys going back out, or do you want to wait here?"

Vicki yawned, shifting her weight so that she was snuggled against Shay in Mark's absence. "Stay here."

"Fine with me," Shay said with a rueful smile. "I wasn't exactly hitting my stride tonight. You go on, we'll be waiting."

So Mark assisted Heather in coaxing her nervous friend out on the floor. Once there, the girl kept a death grip on the gold bar until she ran out of railing.

"We'll hold your hands," Heather volunteered, putting the girl between herself and Mark. After their first complete circle, the other girl gained a smidge of confidence—not enough to actually let go of any-one's hand; Mark was losing circulation in a few of his fingers—enough to speed up slightly. As they coasted into a turn, however, the girls got too close together, bumping into each other. Somehow, the wheels of their roller skates interlocked. Heather's friend panicked, and, with a sinking realization in the pit of his stomach, Mark knew they were all going down.

Instead of letting go and abandoning the girls to fend for themselves, he did his best to control the landing. At the last minute, he instinctively put his hand out to brace them, even though, rationally, he knew better. The pain was blade-sharp and immediate. Wrists were more delicate than people realized. His had not been intended to absorb the weight of a grown man and two toppling third graders.

Because the floor was so much emptier than it had been earlier in the evening, other skaters easily gave them a wide berth. The girls needed help standing, and unfortunately, Mark didn't think he could manage that one-handed.

"A little assistance here?" he called out loudly, to be heard over the music.

Even though it was against house rules, Charlotte Wilkes hurried out onto the rink floor in her sneakered feet. "Mark! Are you all right? Girls?"

"We're fine, Mom," Heather answered, while her friend grumbled, "*This* is why I didn't wanna skate. I told you I'd suck."

"Do you need a hand, too?" Charlotte asked him while the girls made their way off the floor.

"Maybe." He held up the hand that wasn't cradled painfully to his body, glad she wasn't wearing skates anymore. The last thing he wanted was to topple the diminutive woman. For a second, his wrist had hurt badly enough that little black dots danced in front of his eyes. Though the pain hadn't faded, the shock of it was easing. He got a clear look at Vicki and Shay staring at him. Their matching worried expressions made them look comically alike even though their features were so dissimilar.

"Daddy?" Vicki's voice was tremulous and Mark knew that when she was this tired it didn't take much to make his little girl cry.

"I'll be okay." Which might have been more convincing if he could stop grimacing in agony. *Damn,* his hand hurt.

Shay kept her voice discreetly lowered. "It's bad, isn't it?"

"Yeah." He thought he might have heard a cracking sound when he hit the floor, but it was hard to be sure over the pop song that had been playing and the internal *Ow!* that had roared through his body. Along with a few choice words he could not repeat in front of Vicki.

"I am so sorry," Charlotte said, obviously suffering guilt that he'd been injured in the line of helping her daughter's friend. "Heather, go get Mr. Hathaway some ice from concessions."

"Yes, ma'am." The third grader zoomed off in the other direction, while her friend stayed behind, untying her skates as fast as she could and apologizing every few seconds.

"Vicki, honey, why don't you sit with Tessa for a minute?" Charlotte directed. Then she asked Mark, "Do you think you should get an X-ray?"

He wanted to tell her that was probably overkill, but his wrist was already visibly swelling.

Shay nodded insistently. "There are twenty-seven

bones in the hand. You might have broken one or more of them. I can drive you to the hospital if Charlotte needs to get her daughters home. Something like a quarter of E.R. visits are for broken wrists," she added absently.

He almost managed a laugh. "Were you a health teacher?"

"Biology. But I also helped my brother, Dr. Morgan, study for the MCAT."

"Well, I don't have any direct relations to a doctor," Charlotte said, "but even I know wrists shouldn't be that color. We'll take Vicki home with us and she can spend the night. If all else fails, she can wear Tessa's clothes tomorrow. They're near enough to the same size."

Mark frowned about the disruption to everyone's schedules and routine, but didn't get the chance to object.

Charlotte put her hands on her hips. She was tiny, but fierce. "Don't you argue with me, Mark Hathaway. Vicki only has one parent, so it's your responsibility to take extra good care of yourself."

When she put it that way…

SHAY KNEW SHE WAS BABBLING like an idiot—well, an idiot with a medical degree—and thought that Mark was showing great patience in not asking her to shut up. As she drove them toward the hospital, she'd told him that he might be looking at a Colles' fracture, explained what the first-aid acronym RICE stood for—Rest, Ice, Compression, Elevation—and had been asking if he had any known allergies to medication.

He finally chuckled, although it was clear from the tension in his face that his wrist was still hurting. "You know, I plan on being conscious when we check me into the E.R. It's not necessary for you to have my complete medical history memorized. But just in case I do lose consciousness…my health insurance card is in my back pocket. You have my permission to look for it," he invited.

She slanted him a suspicious look. "I can't tell if you're being helpful or flirting with me."

"Then I must be really bad at flirting. Ignore me. The pain is clouding my judgment." He grated his teeth. "I can't believe I did this to my wrist. The thing is, I know better. I've done hiking and some low-intensity mountain climbing—they always tell you not to catch yourself with your hand like that."

"Don't beat yourself up. Knowing something in the abstract isn't the same as being caught in the moment." For instance, she knew better than to ever do anything unprofessional at a school function where dozens of parents could witness it, but there'd been a moment tonight—over by the concessions, with Mark staring down into her eyes—where, heaven help her, she'd wanted to kiss him. *Idiot*. The man had a daughter who was obsessed with finding a new mommy, for crying out loud. If Vicki saw her dad in a lip-lock with someone, she'd be hearing wedding bells in her head.

And who knew what narrow-minded people like Carolyn Moon might think?

They could assume Shay was a loose woman who didn't think twice about jumping into bed with a man she'd only known a couple of weeks. The truth was, Shay hadn't been in anyone's bed in…geez, it had been so long she couldn't really keep track. But Shay spent all day around impressionable children. The perception of herself that she presented, as a role model, was almost as important as the truth.

"You know how people joke that something's so easy they can do it with one hand tied behind their backs?" he asked tiredly. "I hope that proves true of returning the store to profitability and leading the Campside Girls."

She bit her lip, thinking that this could definitely hamper his arts-and-crafts abilities. "If it helps, they probably won't actually tie your hand behind your back. They'll probably go with a splint or cast. And we're going to put out a call for volunteers to help you with the girls. Just because no one wanted to take charge doesn't mean they won't be willing to assist."

Especially when some mothers at the school learned that the troop leader was an extremely handsome, extremely eligible man.

Once they reached the hospital, Shay struggled to find a parking space. Apparently Tuesday nights at nine-thirty were prime time for accidents, injuries and illnesses. Finally—*hallelujah*—she located a spot and ushered Mark inside. Even though he'd injured his left hand, not the one he wrote with, she offered to fill out the forms for him.

The place was packed, with very few chairs free. When Shay spotted a lone seat, she gestured toward it with the clipboard the woman at the desk had given them. "You should sit."

"No." Mark eyed the chair as if it were a venomous copperhead poised to strike.

Men. "The attempt at chivalry is appreciated," she said, "but unnecessary. Next time, when I'm the one injured and you have to bring me to the hospital, we can reverse roles."

Silver lightning flashed in his eyes, but he didn't say anything else, merely shook his head.

"All right," she relented, surprised by this cranky side of Mark but reminding herself what a pain Bastien had always been when he was sick. Her mother used to joke that this was why women were the ones who endured pregnancy and giving birth, because men were such babies—no pun intended—about being patients. "I'll fill this out and then see about getting you fresh ice."

"Here." Mark awkwardly angled his good hand behind him, then held out his wallet. "License, social security card, health insurance. Get what you can off those, then let me know what other information you need."

"All right." Eventually she did sit, because it made flipping through his wallet and writing easier. She copied his address and full name from his license and smiled at his April birth date. "Hey, we're both Aries."

He grunted, looking around the room and not meeting her eyes.

She thought about what he'd told her of his boss and Coleridge's impending spring decision; she couldn't help thinking that *not* closing the store would make a fantastic birthday gift. The pen in her fingers wobbled just a bit over the section where it asked about marital status. She quickly checked widowed, suddenly feeling strange about this, answering personal questions about a man who'd once had a wife. Jess had probably done this for him at some point in their marriage. Or maybe the reverse was true—had he brought Jessica to the hospital when Vicki was born, filled out all the medical forms with anxious joy, hoping that everything went well and looking forward to meeting his new daughter?

Shay had finished with all the straightforward blanks and was getting his answer for each individual question under the family history section when a nurse came forward and called his name.

Shay walked forward with him and handed the woman the paperwork. The nurse smiled at her. "Are you the wife? Girlfriend?"

"No!" Mark answered for her. "She's just the woman who drove me here."

It was nothing more than the truth.

Then why, Shay wondered as she watched him go down the hall, had hearing him say it hurt so much?

Chapter Eight

"I-owe-you a 'pology." Mark's words ran together, his breath forming foggy puffs of air in the cold parking lot. "For before." He snickered, then said it again. "*For before*. Sounds funny."

Shay felt like smacking herself in the forehead except that both of her hands were fully occupied trying to maneuver him into the car. "Whatever meds the doc gave you, it was the good stuff."

The nurse who'd returned Mark to the waiting room a little more than an hour after he'd gone back explained that he had a bad sprain. According to the X-rays, no bones were broken. They'd given him a painkiller and immobilized the wrist for now. The doctor had attached a list of exercises to the prescription sheet; if Mark felt up to it, he was supposed to try the rehab exercises in the next few days. They were anticipating a full recovery in three to six weeks as long as he was careful in the meantime.

But Mark didn't seem to care overly much about his prognosis. When he'd come back through those doors, his somewhat unfocused eyes had been searching for her. "Shay! So glad I found you."

She hadn't known she was lost. "Right here waiting," she'd said. "Let's get you home."

As they'd made their way out of the hospital, she'd realized he was genuinely agitated.

"Couldn't stop thinkin' about you," he told her. "Was an ass earlier."

She'd tried not to recall how irrationally wounded she'd been by his brusque dismissal. "Don't worry about it. You were just cranky because you were in pain. No big deal."

Despite her forgiveness, he kept trying to apologize all the way to the car. And now, even when they'd reached their destination, he continued the litany.

"It's hospitals," he slurred, "that make me cranky. Haven't been in one…since Jess."

"Oh." She wasn't sure what to say to that, but it did help explain why he'd been in such a bad mood when they went into the E.R. She'd chalked it up to physical discomfort and the general unpleasantness of having to wait around in a throng of miserable people.

"She was sick," he said as he folded himself into the passenger seat. "Rare cancer, late stage. Too late. Hate hospitals," he repeated bleakly, looking up at her from inside the car.

Shay reached out her hand to lay it on his shoulder, wanting to offer even a millisecond of comfort, anything to combat the ugly memories.

He surprised her by catching her fingers in his good hand and pressing her palm against his face, covering it with his own. Though he didn't have a visible five-o'clock shadow, she could feel the slightest bristles against her skin. He turned his head slightly, his breath hot on her flesh. Shay's pulse kicked into a gallop.

When he spoke, his voice was still thick with medically administered narcotics, but his eyes seemed clearer. "Almost kissed you earlier tonight."

Her breath froze in her lungs and she had to force herself to exhale. *Almost let you.* "I know."

"Probably shouldn't?"

Shay couldn't tell whether it was a statement or a question. But she answered it as much for her own good as his. "Probably not."

AFTER GETTING MARK'S EXACT address from his license, Shay thought she had a pretty good idea of where he lived. Apparently, she'd been wrong.

Since Mark had drifted to sleep before she'd even cleared the ticket booth in the hospital's parking deck, he hadn't been much help. She'd opted not to wake him—as much from self-preservation as out of kindness. On a feminine, instinctive level, she'd been aware of the chemistry between them, those moments that were a little too charged to be fully platonic, the glances that lasted a smidge too long to be casual. But she hadn't expected him to bring it into conversation so candidly. Now that he had, it was more difficult to act as if those sparks weren't there.

Almost kissed you. She shivered. What would that have been like, kissing Mark Hathaway?

"Pull yourself together," she muttered in the dark car. Good grief, no wonder she'd gotten herself lost on Braeden's back roads. It was difficult to fantasize and pay attention to where you were driving at the same time. Time to enlist help. "Mark?"

Nothing. He was out—not snoring, not fidgeting in his sleep, but finally, completely untroubled. His face was expressionless and unlined, his eyelashes dark crescents against his cheeks. Although she'd seen him laughing before, picking on Cade or grinning at his daughter, she realized now that even when Mark was having fun, there was a subtle tension in the way he held himself. This was the first time she'd seen him at peace.

In Vicki's Valentine solicitation, she'd said that her dad was lonely. Shay wondered if he felt that way. Though he obviously had friends and family who cared a great deal for him, at the end of the day, he still had to shoulder his responsibilities alone.

Like you. Shay was comfortably independent and a proud feminist. She didn't "need" a man, and her parents' insinuations that she did had rubbed her nerves raw. But she had to admit, there were days that just sucked out loud, when school boards voted in bad policies that principals then had to implement whether they agreed with them or not, days where you went home knowing that despite your efforts you hadn't gotten through to a child with the message you wanted them to hear—and on those days, a friendly hug or back rub or even a heartfelt "you did the best you could" would count for a lot. And in the running of his store and raising of his daughter, Mark didn't have that, either.

She might have experienced a twinge of pity for him, except that would have equaled feeling sorry for herself, too, which she refused to do.

"Mark!" Her voice was louder, more demanding this time.

He inhaled deeply, blinking as he slowly came awake. "Shay?" He seemed confused by his surroundings.

Her name sounded far different in Mark's sleepy

drawl. "Y-yeah. I'm taking you home from the E.R., remember? Only I think we took a wrong turn."

Straightening in his seat, he looked out the window. "Where the hell are we?"

"Not entirely sure. That's what I meant by *wrong turn.*" In her defense, she'd only lived in town a month—most of which had been spent at the school, her house, or Geneva's—it was dark, and it was going on midnight. Her mental acuity for the day had peaked hours ago.

"Okay, give me a sec. Can you pull over, let me get my bearings?"

They had the road completely to themselves. It was no trouble to steer her car over to the shoulder. She tried to talk him through the roads she'd taken.

"Got it, you should have gone left on Gideon instead of a right. And you must have taken Pine Street."

"Isn't that what I wanted?"

"Nope. Our subdivision is off Pine Court."

She scowled. "The town ain't that big. How many *pines* do they really need?"

"Well, it is the state tree," he teased gently. "As long as there's no one coming, let's make a U-turn. I'll let you know when to turn."

Glancing in her side mirrors, she spun the wheel. "You're obviously feeling more...alert. How's the hand?"

"Throbbing. I don't know if I remembered to say so earlier, but thanks for taking me to the hospital. I really didn't want to go, but it was the right call."

He'd brought up his wife before he'd fallen asleep. Would it help him to talk about it? Keeping her voice matter-of-fact, the way she did with parents or students who had been through something traumatic, she asked,

"Did you guys have to spend lots of time in the hospital when Jessica got sick?"

"Not enough." He sounded calm, not as maudlin as he had in his pharmaceutical haze. "She had such non-specific symptoms that she didn't go to the doctor for a long time. Even when she did, it took them too long to identify a cancer that had already spread from its original site. So we didn't spend months and years in and out of the hospital the way some people do, which is probably a mercy. But since her diagnosis was so grim from the beginning, the trips we did make were all… It was awful to be in a place that's supposed to be about healing and recovery and not have any hope."

She wanted to tell him she was sorry, but they were just words. Inadequate and redundant—she was sure he'd heard it a hundred times.

"Losing her was even more difficult than when my parents died," he said. "My folks died a couple of years apart, obviously not as young as Jess was, and she's the person who helped me cope with their deaths. When she died— It's melodramatic to say I felt utterly alone. After all, Dee had just lost her sister, which had to hurt like hell, yet she still found the strength to take care of me and Vicki."

"Is Vicki a lot like her mom?" Shay asked, helping him focus on the bright spot in his life. "No offense, but I couldn't help noticing she looks nothing like you."

"She's definitely her mother's daughter, but Jess was…sweet. Soft. That makes her sound weak, doesn't it? She wasn't. She just didn't have my ornery streak. Vicki does. My daughter has a big heart—I've never seen her do anything intentionally malicious—but she can be seriously stubborn."

Shay chuckled, recalling the little girl's determined face as she'd announced that "people should never give up." "There are worse things to be in life. A sense of persistence might serve her well."

"Let's hope I can redirect that 'persistence' to earning Campside Girls badges instead of marrying me off!"

"Do you think you'll ever get married again?" The question escaped of its own volition, hanging over them like one of those cartoon dialogue bubbles. It was none of Shay's business and it would be easy to mistake her curiosity for personal interest. Yet since she'd already put it out there, she held her breath, waiting to see if he would answer.

"I don't know," he said. "Maybe? It's not that I've decided to be alone forever. Or even that I'm waiting to be 'over' her. I loved Jessica. She gave me Vicki. She'll always be part of who I am. But she wouldn't want me to spend my life as some untouchable shrine to what we had. I just… I don't think much about it."

"You have plenty of other things on your mind," Shay said. She knew what that was like. Her mother had seemed to believe for a couple of years that Shay was deliberately avoiding relationships in rebellion against her parents. But Shay had friends and a job and commitments in the community—unconsciously rebelling was only a tiny fraction of her motivation.

"If I ever did stop to imagine it," Mark continued, "well, it's tough to see anyone else as my wife. Hell, it's hard to picture anyone else as a girlfriend. She was the only one I ever had."

Shay almost swerved off the road. "You're kidding."

"We were high school sweethearts. I went out on a

few dates before we met, held hands with a girl in middle school and called it 'going together,' but my only real relationship was Jess."

Wow.

"I sound wildly inexperienced, don't I?"

It was a loaded question. Judging from his heated gaze as he'd looked into her eyes at the skating rink, Shay would have said he was a man who knew exactly what he was doing and what he wanted. "N-not exactly."

Just because he'd been committed to one woman and didn't take relationships lightly...well, that was kind of sexy, actually. Geneva had admitted on the phone that Cade's local reputation was as a charming, free-spirited ladies' man. The two of them had been out and enjoyed each other's company, but Geneva wasn't picking out china patterns. But someone like Mark? If he—

"Here!" His sharp declaration startled her. "We need to turn here. Sorry, should have mentioned that sooner."

She made an abrupt turn, glad there was no one on the road behind them.

"Then you'll make a left at the second stop sign," Mark directed.

"Got it, thanks."

"So what about you?" he asked as she drove. "Leave a string of brokenhearted ex-boyfriends behind you?"

"Just one. I mean, there've been other boyfriends, but only one ever got serious enough that he might have been truly brokenhearted." At least, she liked to imagine him that way. "We were together three and a half years, even got engaged, but I broke it off a few months before we reached the altar."

Mark remained silent, wordlessly encouraging her to

tell the story. It was only fair, she thought. He'd certainly opened up to her.

"I was twenty-two when we met. We were both student teaching, used to have these long discussions about the school system, ways it could be more effective, personal contributions we hoped to make, ideas for improving it. Eventually, he adopted more of a 'why rock the boat?' philosophy, and I was brainstorming my grand ideas alone."

"So you broke up with him because you were an idealist and he was lazy?"

"No. I know I can get…carried away. I grew up doing my homework at the back of my mom's classroom, listening to her and her teacher friends talk. I've always had big plans that get reined in by more conservative boards and, you know, reality. It probably made sense for me to be with someone a little less zealous. What bothered me was the day when I was ranting and raving about a standardized testing policy I thought could hurt more kids than it ended up helping and Bryan joked, 'Well, if it bothers you so much, you can just homeschool our kids.' Plenty of families choose homeschooling as a valid alternative, but that's not where I belong. Or what I ever wanted. When we got to talking more about it, I realized he actually could picture me at home with our kids, setting aside my career even though I was more passionate and ambitious about mine than he was about his. Does that make me sound selfish?" she asked, ashamed that she was seeking the validation. Her mother had thrown a fit when Shay broke the engagement.

"Selfish because you didn't want to marry someone who clearly didn't understand you? Or share your life goals?" Mark shook his head. "You're a bright, beautiful woman who deserves to be loved for who she is. Why settle for someone who's a poor fit when you would have made each other miserable?"

Her lips parted in surprise at his eloquent flattery. "Th-thank you. I would love for you to meet my mother someday. Maybe you could get her to come around to your way of thinking."

They'd made it back to an area of town Shay recognized, and finding the rest of the way was easy.

Even with the streetlight, she couldn't tell much about the outside of his house in the dark. It was slightly bigger than hers, some toy horses sat up on the porch, and the lawn definitely needed to be cut.

"This is it," Mark said, awkwardly removing his seat belt with one hand.

"Could you use some help unlocking the front door? Or assistance with anything inside?"

His eyes met hers, inscrutable. Then he shook his head. "I'll manage, but thanks. You've done more than enough for me tonight. Have dinner with me on Valentine's Day," he blurted.

"What?" She couldn't tell from the way he'd said it if it was a completely impulsive invitation or if it was something he'd simply been too nervous to say until now.

"As…as a thank-you for everything."

She tried to wave away the gratitude. "It was an emergency situation. I would have done the same for any of my parents." Probably.

"I already know you don't have plans," he cajoled. "You told me you didn't. We don't have to go out—I understand that people might get the wrong idea. Why not come here? You, me and Vicki. We'll cook out. I know Vicki says I'm a lousy chef, but I can grill with the best of them."

A laugh burbled out of her. "In the middle of February, one of the coldest months of the year?"

"Come on, Principal Morgan." He flashed a grin. It wasn't his legendary stubbornness that was going to get her; it was the undeniable pull in those gray eyes. "Live a little."

Chapter Nine

"No, Ed, to the left!"

"Your left, or my left?" the young man on the ladder asked.

"We're facing the same way! We don't have different lefts!" Mark didn't mean to snap at his employee. He was frustrated that he only had mobility in one hand, which made decorating the store for the upcoming Valentine's Day sale difficult. So he'd been relegated to supervising a guy who could calculate sales tax in his head better than anyone else in the county but was color-blind, lacked depth perception and apparently couldn't hang anything level to save his life.

This morning, Ed had been out distributing fliers about the big weeklong sale until a rainstorm drove him back to the store. The pounding rain was supposed to trail off and turn to sleet once the sun began setting this afternoon. Mark crossed his fingers that the roads would be clear tomorrow. He had that drive to make to Hawk Summit. The operations manager had agreed to donate one night's stay for a couple, to be raffled off at Mark's store.

"It's pretty romantic up here," the man had told him on the phone, "if I do say so myself. The exterior rooms have some spectacular views, and the luxury suites feature deluxe, Whirlpool bathtubs and his-and-her robes."

A deal like that could certainly help make someone's Valentine's Day special.

Mark thought again of Shay's parting words when she'd left him the night before last. *I'll think about it.* Was she truly considering joining him for Valentine's Day, or had that simply been her polite way of dodging the question? He'd shocked her with the invitation.

Of course, he'd also shocked himself.

Perhaps he'd been spurred to action by the conversation they'd had earlier, when he'd told her he didn't really want to be alone—yet wasn't he? Or maybe his judgment had been clouded by achiness, exhaustion and medicine, resulting in uncharacteristic behavior. But most likely his question came from really, really wanting to see her again.

Mark wasn't to the point of actually hoping Vicki would get in trouble just so he would get called to Shay's office, but that wasn't outside the realm of future possibility. Mark groaned. How had he become so far gone?

"What, it's still not in the right place?" Ed demanded, scowling at the large sign he was attempting to hang. Obviously, he'd misinterpreted the disgruntled noise his boss had made.

"No, the banner's fine now. Sorry, I was just— I'd better get that," Mark interrupted himself when the phone rang. "Up A Creek. Mark Hathaway speaking."

"Mark, it's Shay Morgan." Suddenly, his hand hurt less and his day shone brighter, even through the thunderclouds dipping over the store.

"I was just thinking about you," he said. Was that too blunt, too needy?

"Oh?" Her voice went breathless. "What about?"

Maybe the admission hadn't been needy after all. He swore he could hear her pleased blush—he'd noticed more than once that her delicate skin flushed easily. She had such fair coloring, almost disarmingly fragile for a woman so strong.

"Valentine's Day," he said, stifling mental images of Whirlpool bathtubs. "Let me guess, you're calling to accept my offer. Valentine's Day is on a Monday. How late do you usually stay at the school? We'll plan dinnertime around your schedule."

"That's not actually why I called." But she sounded as if she were smiling.

"Well, then you can kill two birds with one stone. Solidify our plans *and* discuss whatever you called about."

"You're very—"

"Persistent," he supplied unrepentantly. "I'm told there are worse things to be in life."

"Fine, I'll be there at six-thirty. Will that work?"

Mark wasn't fooled by her mock-grudging tone. Nobody pushed around Shay Morgan. If she said yes, it was because she wanted to be with him. Eagerness suffused him. It felt as if he hadn't looked forward to a Valentine's Day in a lifetime, yet he couldn't wait for this one.

"So, what else can I do for you, Principal Morgan?"

"Check your email, please. I drafted a letter for the parents of prospective Campside Girls and just sent it to you. It gives the details of how to sign up and also asks for willing volunteers. I just wanted to get your input before I ask Roberta to print copies and put them in the teachers' boxes."

"Will do." He shot a glance toward Ed, who was easily within earshot, and lowered his voice. Mark liked to maintain some degree of competence in front of employees. "Shay, you're not…I don't know, worried about me being troop leader, are you?"

"What do you mean? I told you all the necessary people were on board with it. Hasn't the regional leader been in touch?"

"Yeah, I know everything's in order, officially. But to recap, I volunteered to read to first graders and you ended up with parental complaints. I volunteered to help with the skate night and I ended up in the E.R."

She stifled a laugh. "I see your point. But you're missing the larger picture. You've encountered difficulties and you keep coming back anyway. And you took the brunt of that fall, protecting those two girls. I wish we had more parents like you at Woodside."

"Then you're out of luck—I think I'm one of a kind." He'd tried to make a joke but, strangely self-conscious over her praise, his voice was gruff.

She hesitated, agreed softly, "Yes, you are."

"MOST PEOPLE KNOCK WITH their fist," Geneva remarked wryly. "Not their forehead. You want to tell me why you're standing on my front porch banging your head on the door?"

"Last-ditch attempt to knock some sense into myself," Shay said. It was Thursday evening. They were planning to order a veggie pizza and a couple liters of diet soda, then plop down in Gen's living room to watch a Hugh Jackman movie.

"Hang on, I'll go get a baseball bat and help."

"Ha-ha." Shay hung her jacket on the rack in the foyer. "It is to laugh."

"Well, Cade appreciates my sense of humor." Geneva sniffed, pretending to be offended—an effect she completely ruined with her self-satisfied grin. "Course, that's not all he appreciates."

"You may not be the only one with an admirer," Shay said. "Mark asked me to have dinner with him on Valen—"

"I knew it!" Geneva whooped. "I told you the night of the town council meeting that the two of you had chemistry. Didn't I tell you?"

"Before you get all carried away, it's dinner at his house with his six-year-old daughter as de facto chaperone, so—"

"What are you going to wear?"

"I don't know." Shay blinked at her. "I only agreed to it a couple of hours ago. And I've been having second thoughts ever since."

"Second thoughts? Why, because— Wait, come with me." Geneva spun on her heel and headed for the kitchen. "We need wine. White, or red?"

"What happened to the guilt-free diet soda?"

"Please. Good gossip requires wine." Geneva was already pulling blue-stemmed glasses down from a cabinet. "Besides, we should toast the occasion. Your first date in Braeden, finally!"

In the refrigerator door, Shay found an already opened bottle of Italian pinot grigio.

"So why the doubts?" Geneva asked as she poured. "Is it because you think he's still too hung up on his wife to be in a healthy relationship?"

"Actually, no. He loved her a lot, but I don't see that as being an impediment to his getting involved again. They had a great marriage. Mark's not one of those jaded men who's been burned and doesn't even realize how angry he still is."

Geneva pulled a face. "Dated that guy."

"Mark's got other complications, though. Work stress," she said, keeping it vague since he'd asked her not to tell people about the fate of the store hanging in the balance. "But more importantly, his little girl. He has to worry does Vicki like the woman, does Vicki like the woman too much? What if she gets attached and it doesn't work out? And then there's…"

"Yes?"

"Well, I think he's been reserved because he doesn't have any practice dating."

"You mean he's out of practice because he was married for years."

"No, I mean his wife is the only woman he dated."

"Get out!" Geneva's eyebrows shot up. "So was she the only woman he…? And they had years to get it right."

"Geneva!" Shay choked on her wine. "What is wrong with you?"

"Many things. But for him to share such an intimate history with one person—and only one person—that kind of puts pressure on the next lady."

"Stop looking at me like that," Shay said, blood rushing to her cheeks. "We're having dinner with his daughter, not running off for a romantic weekend at the Biltmore."

"So you've never thought about it? Not even once?" her friend challenged, the gleam in her eyes devilish.

"What, the Biltmore? No, I can't afford that on my salary. Where's the number for the pizza delivery place? I'm starving."

Geneva chuckled into her wineglass. "Yeah. That's what I thought."

"ALL THIS AND GREAT FOOD, too?" Mark sat back in his chair, trying to remember when he'd had a more satisfying lunch than the one he'd just enjoyed in the Hawk Summit main dining room. The furniture might be deliberately rustic-looking, but the cuisine was top-notch. "This place is fantastic, and I'm not just saying that because I want to do business with you."

Across the table, Jeffrey Frye, the operations manager, laughed. "Thank you. We started with such grand plans, but we hit a snag with zoning and then construction and by the time we opened…" He looked around forlornly at the dining room, which wasn't even a quarter full.

"Tough economy," Mark commiserated. "I can't help you with national advertising or anything, but there's something to be said for word of mouth, a grass-roots approach. It's a start, anyway. I've put together some advertising ideas in here to use in Braeden—I have a vested interest in regional outdoor recreation, obviously—but feel free to tweak it and use it in other outlying towns."

"That's damn decent of you." Jeffrey flipped through the red folder. "Some of these are better than what the marketing consults we paid gave us."

Mark was going to heavily promote the new resort in town and through his store. In return, for customers who brought receipts showing they'd bought outerwear and ski gear from Up A Creek, Jeffrey had agreed that for the rest of this year's ski season, he'd give a half-off discount on lift tickets or a fifteen percent discount on a room at the main lodge, availability permitting. In addition to the rooms at the lodge, there were two separate smaller hotels on the property, one that catered to families and one that was exclusively for adults. It was a stay in that building which was being raffled at the conclusion of Mark's Valentine's Day sale, and Jeffrey had taken him on a brief tour of the romantic inn.

Everywhere Mark had turned, he'd seen Shay. He could picture her relaxing in the chair by the fireplace, laughing at a day's efforts on the slopes. Was she better on skis than skates? He'd envisioned her rolling her shoulders and declaring she needed a soak beneath the Jacuzzi-style jets. And he hadn't dared glance in the direction of the king-size bed.

"You married, seeing anyone special?" Jeff had asked amiably.

Mark had started to tell him no, but the words that had come out were, "Maybe. It's a little soon to tell," he'd added, sounding far too boyish for a grown man who'd driven up here with business propositions to make.

Jeff had grinned. "Well, keep us in mind should it turn into anything serious. The main lodge can also accommodate small weddings."

Mark, forcefully pushing aside thoughts of Shay, wondered if the Campside Girls and their parents might want to come up for a family weekend of snow-tubing before the slopes closed at the end of March. On the drive back to Braeden, he thought more about the Campside Girls. Letters had gone home yesterday and sign-up for the troop was supposed to take place next week.

He knew that Vicki's friends Val and Tessa were both

interested and that their mothers seemed to trust him to know what he was doing—more fools, they. Would he get many takers beyond that? He didn't know which concerned him more, no one joining and the "troop" being deemed a dismal failure or more girls participating than he could possibly handle.

Before he reached town, he needed to make a slight detour to a regional Campside Girls headquarters to purchase supplies and a leadership packet. He could also get Vicki's handbook and uniform; the rest would have to be ordered by individual parents. The receptionist at the administrative building was a grandmotherly type who proudly wore a Campside Girls butterfly pin on her blouse and waved him inside. She turned him over to a "Miss Temple" for assistance, a pretty dark-haired woman with a friendly smile and dimples.

"A male Campside Girl—very novel," she teased as she dug through a huge set of double cabinets for all of the paperwork he needed. "Did you have a mom or big sister in the program, someone who sparked your interest?"

"That would be my six-year-old daughter," he answered.

"Most girls talk their mamas into leading a troop."

"Vicki's mother passed away a couple of years ago, so she just has me."

"Well, bravo to you for stepping in. And if you need any help—have any questions—you just give us a call." She pulled a business card out of her blouse pocket. "This has my direct number. I could even come out to the school if you want help with parent orientation or need some backup at an event."

By the time he returned to the front of the building

to pay for Vicki's stuff, Miss Temple had made several more offers to drive out to Braeden and assist him. It occurred to him, distantly, that she might even like him. She wouldn't be the first woman over the past two years who'd expressed some degree of interest. He'd rarely felt a reciprocal flare and yet, whenever he was within ten feet of Shay…

I want her. The thought was still so new that it was mildly shocking. Walking out to his car, he glanced around, semiguiltily, as if people could take one look at him and know he harbored lustful desires. What would she do if he acted on one of them, something as basic as a kiss?

He wasn't sure. But even if she felt differently, he was grateful to her. When she'd asked him about romance in his life, he'd told her that he simply couldn't picture being with anyone else. That part of him had been dormant for a long time, but she'd changed that. She'd invigorated him, helped him feel whole again.

Now he just had to figure out what to do about it.

AFTER SEVERAL ROUNDS OF POKER at Mark's kitchen table Friday night, he knew that Cade was perfectly capable of keeping his face blank. There was no outward sign of humor in the other man's impassive expression. But the mirth in the big man's voice was downright deflating.

"Just to clarify," Cade said, "exactly what kind of advice are you looking for here?"

Mark glared. "Never mind. And if you say, 'It's just like riding a bike,' you're going to be wearing your beer." He stood, clearing the empty bowls that had earlier held chips and salsa. He should probably also go carry his daughter into her room. Vicki had fallen asleep on the couch watching *The Sound of Music* for probably the hundredth time. He was going to have that yodeling goatherd song stuck in his head all weekend.

Peeking around the corner, he grinned at the picture she made. Over top of long, footed pajamas featuring rainbow-colored ponies, she wore her brand-new Campside Girls vest. The beret sat crookedly across her head, her curly hair a reddish explosion against the beige couch cushion. One arm was draped over her face, the other flung straight back, still holding her stuffed horse, Pinky.

"Quite a picture," Cade said fondly. "Want me to take her down the hall for you? The last thing you need is to make that wrist any worse. Get healed so we can go back to our weekly basketball games at the rec center. It's not the same playing Rockwell. I beat both of you, but he hardly presents enough of a challenge to make it worth my time."

"Yeah, you're all talk now, when I can't even hold the ball with both hands," Mark scoffed. He went down the hall ahead of his friend, making sure there were no toys to trip over and no talking stuffed animals that would start making noise whenever they sensed motion. Then he bent to plug in Vicki's barn-shaped night-light in case she woke up in the middle of the night. He kissed his daughter on the forehead and tucked Pinky securely in the crook of her arm.

Once both men had tiptoed back out of her room, Cade asked, "Have you told her yet, about your Big Date?"

"Stop calling it that. And no. I figured I'd tell her closer to the actual day. I don't want her to spend the next week and a half building up its significance in her head."

"It *is* pretty significant, though—all kidding aside. I'm impressed as hell that you asked her out. Isn't this the first date you've been on that someone didn't either set up for you or twist your arm to make? And Valentine's Day, no less! The most romantic day of the year, when women's expectations are high? No pressure."

Mark's stomach flip-flopped. "I hadn't really thought of it like that." Valentine's Day had just seemed like a convenient excuse, since she'd lamented that the height of her day might be getting an exercise ball for her friend. "What about you and Geneva, any big plans?"

"I don't know. Maybe something casual, a movie or ice-skating."

"A little tip? If you fall, don't try to catch yourself with your hand."

Cade gave him a withering look. "Dude, *I* don't fall."

It was on the tip of Mark's tongue to ask if Cade and Geneva wanted to join them here for Valentine's Day, make it more of dinner party than an intimate date. But he recognized that temptation for what it was: cowardice. If Mark was going to dive back into the world of dating, then he was going to do it from the high-dive, seize the moment, no reservations—not use his friends as water wings to keep him afloat.

"DECENT TURNOUT, BOSS." Roddy surveyed the store with satisfaction. "I think the Valentine's angle worked nicely. Getting recreational equipment so that two people can spend even more time in each other's company is an inspired romantic spin. Why didn't we do this last year?"

Because he'd been deliberately oblivious to Valentine's existence, Mark admitted to himself. "Well, cross your fingers. Maybe we can make this an annual event. Now, if you'll excuse me, I see Lydia Fortnaut."

Roddy smirked. "Gonna go help her with more fishing equipment?"

"No, I'm going to hide in the supply closet," Mark said, only half kidding. Thank God Lydia had sons and would not be getting involved with Campside Girls.

With the minor exception of being stalked by occasional rapacious divorcées, Saturday was a moderate success. He wasn't sure whether or not the traffic would continue throughout the week—last-minute shoppers desperate for gift ideas might provide a boost—but he was pleased by the steady stream throughout the day. Even more pleased when the front door opened around three in the afternoon and Shay Morgan stepped inside.

She was pink-cheeked from the cold, her hair pulled into a high bouncy ponytail, and she smiled as soon as she saw him.

He made a beeline straight toward her, hoping his impatience to be near her wasn't patently obvious to everyone else in the store but not caring enough to actually slow down. "Hi."

"Hi back." She glanced around, seeming impressed. "So this is the store. Show me around?"

"Love to. Want to start with exercise stuff? It's a pretty small section, just one aisle." They carried limited basics—yoga mats, weights that could be worn around wrists or ankles and the inflatable exercise balls she'd

mentioned wanting—but Up A Creek was more specialized in outdoor activities.

"No, let's finish our tour with workout supplies. I
want to look at everything else first." She lifted her chin
toward a bike rack. "That stuff's more exotic."

He laughed. "Mountain bikes are exotic?"

"I come from a very bookish family," she admitted.
"My brother and I were more debate team than soccer
team, and all four of us were more likely to be inside
arguing about whether a word counted in Scrabble than
playing lawn golf. I've never once been camping in my
entire life."

"Seriously? That's just plain wrong," he declared.
"Come on, we'll start over in camping goods then."

She arched a brow at the netting that was meant to
keep away bugs and the battery-powered hose contrap-
tion that could be used to convert lake water into an
impromptu shower. Then she looked at Mark as if he
were a lunatic. "Yeah, camping sounds like a riot. Mosquitoes and questionable hygiene—sign me up!"

She paused at an end-cap display of small camping
stoves surrounded by copies of *The Manly Men's Ulti-
mate Foil Cookbook*.

"Don't laugh," Mark said, "some of my most successful grilling recipes have come from that book."

Her teeth sank into her full lower lip. "Is it too late for
me to change my answer about dinner at your place?"

"You wouldn't back out of a promise. You know how
I know?" Mark asked, completely deadpan. "You're far
too *principled*."

Shay groaned, covering her face with her fingers.
"You know how sometimes friends will advise each
other that they need to joke around more? Take it from

someone who cares about you, if those are the best you've got, you should joke around less."

He laughed. "Noted. Speaking of our Valentine's dinner, there's something I... Would you mind stepping in the back with me for a second?"

"Okay." Her turquoise eyes registered curiosity as she nodded. "Nothing's wrong, is it?"

"Just the opposite." He stole a glance around the floor, hoping not to be obvious about the fact that he was taking Shay to his private office.

"Not as fancy as yours," he told her as he shut the door, "but this is where I do my work when I'm not out front."

She picked up one of the framed pictures on his desk. It was one of his favorites, taken when Vicki was three and a half. Jess had purchased matching mother-and-daughter sundresses and had a professional photographer take their picture in the park to give Mark for Father's Day.

"They do look just alike!" Shay said. "Both beautiful." She started to give him the photo to return, and her eyes widened. "I can't believe I haven't asked about your hand yet. You must think I'm completely insensitive."

"Actually, I'd almost forgotten about it myself," he admitted. Her company was the best organic painkiller he knew of. "I'm really glad you came here today."

"Me, too." She smiled, tilting her head back to look up at him as she leaned against the desk. "So, what did you need to...tell me? Show me?"

"Ah, about that." His heart thudded in his chest, picking up speed as he realized he was indeed going through with this. "It was more something I needed to do, before our date."

He took a step closer, unmistakably entering her physical space. Shay's eyes were wide and he could see the flutter of her pulse at the base of her throat.

"Oh?" She licked her bottom lip. "And what was that?"

Bracing his free hand on the cherrywood next to her, he leaned down. "This."

Chapter Ten

Shay was startled, but not alarmed. While she hadn't anticipated being kissed in Mark's office, the last thing she wanted was to pull away. Instead, her eyes drifted closed as she arched up to meet him. His lips were firm and cool on hers. He'd had a peppermint recently. The sweetness was crisp and unexpected. Candy canes and peppermint gum would now hold a completely new association for her.

She'd thought he would be shy, kissing her hesitantly, but she was wrong. His mouth was exactly like that heavy-lidded gaze he'd given her at the roller rink—that of a man who knew what he wanted and how to get it. What he wanted, clearly, was her, and as he deepened their kiss, his tongue stroking hers, she returned that sentiment with every cell in her body. Somehow the fact that he wasn't touching her with either of his hands—one of which he was using for balance, the other splinted between them—made it more erotic.

She was used to men putting their hands around her waist or cupping her face when they kissed her. Missing that was like being unable to see in the dark and having other senses heightened. Without Mark's hands anywhere on her body, she was all the more aware of the other ways they touched. His legs, for instance, had come to bracket hers as he leaned into her. His growing arousal was impossible to miss and made Shay feel deliciously wanton.

Here she was, a bookish academic with no love life to speak of in the past year, making out with a tall, dark and virile man practically atop his desk! She clutched his shirtfront, pulling him even closer but bracing herself against the desk so they didn't lose their balance. She kissed him hungrily, reveling in the sensations he conjured throughout her body, trying to remember why she'd thought he shouldn't kiss her the other night.

She'd been a fool. If a man kissed with Mark's confident mastery, a woman should take advantage of it as often as—

"Mr. Hathaway?" A knock at the office door reverberated through the office like a gunshot.

Shay was so startled that she would have sprung free from his embrace, but there was nowhere to go, trapped as she was against the desk.

"We've got a customer request out here that I need your authority to fulfill," the male voice called through the door.

Mark lowered his head, pressing his forehead to hers and breathing heavily. Even though continuing to touch him probably wouldn't help either of them regain their composure, she couldn't stop herself from running a hand up his back. His muscles were bunched beneath the shirt. Judging from his very fit body, he followed the kind of active lifestyle he encouraged in his customers.

She swallowed as she thought about the strength and stamina that came from keeping active and healthy.

"Be there in a minute, Roddy."

Slowly, Mark straightened, shuffling half a step away from her, as if he needed space but didn't actually want to let her go.

"Do you swim much?" he asked her.

Shay blinked. Of all the things he could have asked at that moment… "Uh, sometimes. In the summer."

"I used to love to go to the community pool and go off the high-dive. It occurred to me that between now and Valentine's Day I was going to be thinking about you. A lot." He gave her a sweetly lopsided smile that made her ache. "And wondering if I should kiss you, thinking about kissing you… It was like getting into the water a centimeter at a time. So when you came in today, I decided I'd take the plunge and see what happened."

Though technically *take the plunge and see what happened* wasn't the most romantic thing any man had ever said to her, Mark had a unique advantage. What had "happened" was spontaneous combustion, the after-effects of which still had her reeling. She didn't care if he compared their kissing to a swan dive, a cannonball or a triple pike as long as they could do it again.

A half groan caught in his chest. "If you keep looking at me like that, I won't be able to leave this office. Shay…"

"No, you should go." She drew a shuddery breath. "We both should. You almost made me forget I've got dinner with my family tonight."

"Is that all?" Mark gave her a grin that was more sinful than anything that had ever been dipped in chocolate or rolled in coconut. "You made me forget my name."

SHAY HUGGED HER MOTHER before shrugging out of her coat. "Sorry I'm late." It was only by a few minutes, but punctuality had always been critical in the Morgan household—as if there was a silent tardy bell only they could hear. But Shay had been running two steps behind all afternoon because she kept losing track of what she was doing, flustered and preoccupied by the lingering memory of that kiss in Mark's office. *Take the plunge indeed.* She felt like she'd yet to come up for air.

"Comparatively speaking, you're early," Pamela Morgan told her. "Bastien called to say his girlfriend's flight back into town was delayed and that we could eat dinner without them if we wanted."

"I'm all right with waiting if you and Dad are." Shay followed her mother through the living room of her past—the sturdy plaid couch had been there for decades. A small set of bookshelves was crowded with spelling bee, debate, science fair and reading bowl trophies. There were no actual books on the rickety living room shelves, but Tom Morgan's study held hundreds of novels, research tomes and his own personal law library.

"Dad in his study?" Shay asked.

Pamela nodded. "He wanted to review some precedents his paralegal found for him, if that's all right. He promised he'd join us when Bastien gets here."

Shay ground her back teeth together. *When Bastien arrives, Dad will grace us with his presence.* Intellectually, she was aware that her flare of annoyance was out of proportion to her dad wanting to squeeze in a little bit more work before dinner. But she'd been conditioned by years of wondering if her dad saw her as a second-class citizen.

"He loves you, you know," Pamela said softly.

Shay started. "Who, Dad? Yeah, I know that." Her mother's insight surprised her, although it shouldn't. After all, Shay's mild resentment—really, she had it under control most of the time—had developed over more than three decades. And her mom had been there to witness each of those decades.

Pamela reached out to pat her cheek. Her fingers, like the rest of her, had aged, but the scent of lavender lotion was the same as it had been through Shay's childhood.

"Come help your mother in the kitchen?" Pamela asked. "I was going to bake a heat-and-serve dessert from the store but when Bastien called, I decided there was time for a homemade apple pie."

"I'll help," Shay volunteered, "but we both know I'm not as good at it as you." Shay actually had a few tasty desserts in her own baking repertoire, but she never managed to make them as cooking-magazine beautiful as her mother.

Pamela had already started slicing green apples at the kitchen island, and Shay picked up where her mother had left off while Pamela worked with the dough.

"You and your brother probably see your father as two separate people," Pamela said. "Bastien thinks his dad has always been too hard on him, and you've no doubt felt as if your dad gave your brother the lion's share of attention. You probably both feel like he loves the other more, but he loves you the same, just differently. He's hard on Bastien because he believes in him."

Shay made a noncommittal sound.

"He believes in you, too. And he's so proud of you. But you were his baby girl, so tiny when you were born, so adorable in your tap recital when you were five."

Adorable might not be the word Shay would

use—she'd seen the picture and was mortified by the giant pink net tutu and the stage makeup that made her look like a miniature Vegas showgirl. She started to remind her mother that she was no longer five, that she was a grown woman with a career she'd worked hard to earn. But then she pictured Mark, already so close to the surface of her thoughts all evening.

She'd watched him with his own little girl, had seen the stress of his knowing he'd never be able to truly protect her from everything that life threw her way, not really. That was a hard pill for a dad to swallow. Maybe some of the suggestions Tom Morgan had made over the years, advice that he saw as making her life easier, had simply been a misguided attempt at protection, not actual chauvinism.

Carefully, she set the knife on the counter and turned to her mom. Shay didn't want to sound accusatory, but she might as well ask this question now instead of spending the next thirty years building unspoken resentment. "What about you, Mom? Why didn't you push me more? I used to think that my going into education would bring us closer together after all your years of teaching. But you've seemed to care more about whether I was dating anyone than whether I was promoted."

Pamela frowned, twin blooms of color appearing on her face. Though Shay and her mom might not resemble each other as blatantly as Vicki Hathaway did her mother, there was no question where Shay had inherited her coloring. And propensity for blushing.

"My love for you isn't conditional on your being 'successful,'" Pamela said. "Promotions are nice, but they're not why I'm proud of you! How shallow do you think I am?"

Oops. "That's not—"

"And as for my asking about your love life, it's because I worry about you! I want you to be happy. A job is not going to bring you soup when you're sick or rub your shoulders when you have a bad day."

Shay bit the inside of her lip. "You're right, Mom."

Pamela's eyebrows shot up. "Well. I wasn't expecting to hear that, but thank you. I may have inspired you to go into education, but I'm not the reason you were a good teacher. Or that you're a good principal. You're good at your job because of how much you care. You have a lot of love to offer, and I guess I always hoped you'd find some man who could appreciate that. When you and Bryan got engaged—"

"He was wrong for me," Shay said decisively.

"I suppose he was, if you chose your career over him. But what if you met someone who was right for you? Would you make the same decision?"

Once again, Mark came to mind. She recalled the empathy in his voice when he'd seconded her decision to break things off with her fiancé, how admiring he seemed to be of how she handled her job—their first meeting notwithstanding. "Mom, I don't think the right man would ask me to make that choice."

MARK STOOD ON THE SMALL cafeteria stage, facing an audience of about a dozen moms and their eager, fidgety daughters. He tapped once to make sure the microphone was still turned safely off before admitting to Shay, "I'm nervous."

Her lips quirked in a grin. "Of a few PTA moms and their little girls?"

"Ha! You know as well as I do that PTA moms can

be dangerous." He didn't mean in the petty, controlling way that Carolyn Moon exemplified. He was talking about the fierce mama-bear quality that he'd glimpsed in his sister-in-law and in Charlotte Wilkes. Charlotte might be tiny, but he had no doubt she'd still find a way to kick the butt of anyone who messed with her kids.

And it had occurred to him that there might come a time when one little girl in his troop hurt the feelings of another or someone fell down during a wilderness hike and some mother would demand to know why he hadn't done more to prevent it.

From the front row, Vicki gave him a thumbs-up, and Mark squashed down his insidious doubts, returning the gesture.

"You'll do great," Shay told him. "Hey, you did well speaking in front of the town council and there are fewer people here. Any luck with the town planner, by the way?"

"More than I expected, actually. I'm not the first person who's approached them about reopening the lodge. A group of women in the historic preservation society tried, since the lodge has roots in our local government, but the building wasn't old enough to qualify for their proposal. And some environmentalists want to reopen the campground to ensure that nothing is built there, marring the area around it. So my timing was fortuitous. The mayor's willing to look at my ideas. He wants to make as many voters as possible happy while also increasing revenue for the town. In the long run, anyway."

There was no denying that it would take an outlay of capital to get the lodge running again, but the nice part was, the lodge was *supposed* to be rustic. Mark was only proposing minor renovations and staffing, not adding a new building or a massive restoration.

Shay favored him with an approving smile. "See? You rock. And I happen to know," she added in a whisper, "you're a phenomenal kisser, so you have that going for you, too."

With an audacious wink, she stepped off the stage and joined his daughter in one of the chairs up front. Mark watched her go. Evil woman. He was supposed to be concentrating on his new duties as troop leader, not the hormones that now threatened to thunder out of control whenever he laid eyes on her.

He cleared his throat and switched on the podium mike. "Good evening. I want to thank you all for coming and thank Principal Morgan for letting us use the cafeteria and for helping make it possible for Woodside Elementary to once again have a Campside Girls troop." He clapped his hands together and the other parents present joined in the brief applause.

"I'm Mark Hathaway and I'm here for the same reason you are—I have a daughter I love. Campside Girls fosters teamwork, environmental awareness, positive self-image and a whole host of other things that I want for Vicki. Some of you have already signed up to join our new troop and I look forward to working with you. For the rest of you, I want to answer any questions you have before you make your decision and tell you a bit about our tentative schedule for the next few months."

He paused, studying his notes. "In late March, we'll have an actual campout, provided I can get a few other adults to sign up, and the Fitness Fair here at Woodside. Participation in that will count toward earning the girls' healthy habits patch."

Earlier in the week, Shay had formally approved Mark's request to have a vendor booth at the fair. He was going to have Roddy run a small rock-climbing wall with the assistance of some high school volunteers to manage the line while Mark supervised a "bike rodeo" and helmet fittings. Even though Keesha had started her new job, she'd said she'd work the booth for a few hours and do free face painting for the kids if Mark would buy the supplies.

Mark talked some more about regular meetings and looking for age-appropriate community service as well as welcoming help from volunteers and ideas for arts-and-crafts projects. The extent of his abilities in that area was to slap some peanut butter on a pinecone, sprinkle seed on it and call it a bird feeder. Although, if it turned out that the Campside Girls had a duct tape badge, he was in business.

When he'd finished covering the information, he asked, "Any questions?" The first hand up belonged to a young woman who looked about college age. "Yes, the lady in blue?"

"Francesca Dover," she said. She bumped shoulders with the little girl sitting next to her. "I'm Deanne's big sister and will probably be bringing her to most of the meetings."

"Wonderful, we look forward to seeing you. And your question is?"

Francesca grinned from ear to ear. "Some of us were wondering—did you ever actually find a Valentine, Mr. Hathaway?"

Muffled titters came from the audience, although most of the moms tried to cover it. One woman in the front clapped a hand over her mouth as if he wouldn't be able to tell she was laughing behind her palm. Wouldn't it shock them all to know he had indeed found a Valentine? It had certainly come as a surprise to him.

Mark studiously did not glance in Shay's direction. He was afraid to single her out, even for a moment. Was she amused by the teasing question, or was she mortified, fighting one of her Technicolor blushes?

He faced down the smirking young woman, returning her smile with effort. "I thank you for your touching concern, Francesca, but we're here for the Campside Girls. Let's not waste time on something as mundane as me. So any other *troop-related* questions?"

When the evening concluded, he had a troop of eight girls, including his daughter.

"Job well done, Mr. Hathaway," Shay congratulated him, her eyes sliding toward his for a brief, private moment before she allowed herself to be separated by a PTA officer who said she needed to ask the principal a favor.

Mark watched her go, wishing they could have had a few minutes alone. He hadn't held her since their kiss in his office, but he'd thought about it every damn day. As eager as he was for their Valentine's dinner on Monday, he had Vicki's presence to consider.

You have to tell her. Usually, people procrastinated giving *bad* news, something they knew would upset the listener. Just the opposite was true in Mark's case. His daughter would likely be jubilant that Shay was joining them for dinner.

From her booster seat in the car, Vicki burbled with excitement about the formation of the troop, especially since Tessa and Valerie had joined. "My best friend and my second-best friend are gonna be with me!"

"Make sure you give the other girls a chance, too," he advised with a quick glance in the rearview mirror. "You'll probably make even more friends."

"You know Deanne?" Vicki asked. It was clearly a rhetorical question, because she instantly followed up with, "Francesca's not really her sister. But Francesca's dad married Deanne's mom, so now they're sisters. If you marry someone with a girl, I can have a mom *and* a new sister!"

Oh, great. His taking on Campside Girls was supposed to help distract Vicki, make her content with the family she already had—namely, him. Instead, she'd upgraded her search from any woman with a pulse to a woman who could provide her a stepsister.

"Victoria, we've talked about this. I might get married someday, a long time from now, but it's not going to happen anytime soon. Please don't try to make it happen."

She slouched down in her seat, scowling. "'Kay."

"I have something to tell you," he began. "I asked a very nice lady to come to our house on Valentine's Day and have dinner with us. Just to be friendly." *And possibly to kiss her senseless after you go to bed.*

"You did? Who? Do I know her?"

"Principal Morgan. Is that okay with you?"

"I *like* her! She told me I was special. And smart. She talked to Mrs. Frost about me and now I get to read to the kindergarten classes sometimes."

He already knew about that. The first time it had happened had been last Friday, and Vicki had come home brimming with excitement and doubled self-esteem. Even if he wasn't crazy about Shay on a personal level, as a parent, he'd be forever grateful that she'd come to the school. Even the lecture she'd given him the first time they'd met had turned out to be in his daughter's best interests.

"I can't believe Principal Morgan is coming over. That's so cool!"

"Cool enough that you'll clean your room before she visits?"

"Do I have to clean all of it?"

"I'll put the stuffed animals back up on the shelf," he offered, knowing it was too high for her to reach without standing on tiptoe atop her bed. Her favorite stuffed animals, like Pinky, held a place of honor on the bed, but Mark had built a shelf that ran the entire length of the wall for her others. "I'll shelve your books, too. But everything else is your responsibility. Deal?"

"Deal!" She looked out the window, whistling tunelessly. It was a recently learned talent, and she'd taken to whistling all the time. But then she stopped to announce, "I can't wait to tell Tessa Principal Morgan is coming to my house."

"I don't know if that's such a good idea, Bug." Although Shay hadn't expressly forbidden him from telling anyone about their dinner date, Mark knew she'd rather keep it under the social radar.

But he didn't want to encourage his daughter to lie to anyone about it, either. "If you start telling kids at school that Principal Morgan is having dinner with us, they might be sad that she isn't coming to their house, too."

"Like bragging? Oh. I don't want Tessa to feel bad." She fell silent. "Daddy..."

"Yes?" He braced himself in case there were any other ethical hurdles he needed to clear.

"Principal Morgan's eating dinner with us?"

"Right." What was she trying to clarify? "Next Monday."

"You should ask Aunt Dee to come help you cook. That way Principal Morgan will want to come back."

Chapter Eleven

In hindsight, Mark wondered if perhaps he shouldn't have taken his daughter's advice and enlisted Dee's assistance. *If all else fails, we can always order a pizza.*

Shay peered at him from over top a glass of red wine, looking hard like she was trying not to smile, lest he take offense. She and Vicki were both seated at the kitchen table, and it was difficult to imagine a prettier tableau. Vicki had wanted to dress up for their guest. She was wearing a pink church dress, her white tights printed with red hearts. She'd accessorized with a headband that featured two more red hearts, sparkly ones, atop springs. Shay had dressed fairly casually in black jeans and a V-neck navy sweater. The soft sweater clung to her curves in a way that made him burn more than the entrée had.

"How's it going over there?" Shay ventured.

If she liked mashed potatoes the consistency of glue, then things were going great. Otherwise…

"Daddy, do you want me to get the pizza magnet off the fridge?" Vicki volunteered. "I could bring you the phone, too."

He sighed, wondering what the wait time was for

delivery. "That's not really what I had in mind for tonight."

Inspired by how much Shay had enjoyed the food at the barbecue house, he'd decided to do barbecue pork ribs. In the spring or summer, he would have fixed them on the grill outside. Given this evening's snow flurries, he'd opted to flame-broil the ribs beneath the oven instead. He'd put Vicki in charge of being "hostess," a role she'd tackled with delight and self-importance, while he cooked. But he'd gotten distracted when he was called in to offer an impartial ruling on the ladies' Uno game; Vicki had long since lost the original box with the rules and the card deck was simply banded together with one of her ponytail holders.

Although Vicki had been known to get upset when her cousin Bobby played cards like "skip" or "draw two" against her, when Shay used the same tactics, Vicki giggled and swore good-natured vengeance. Conversation devolved from playful threats to tickling and the ribs had charred, forgotten.

Still, Mark had been trying to convince himself that if he scraped off some of the black on the outermost part of the ribs, the meat beneath might still be salvageable. That had been before his potatoes gummed up so unappetizingly. Currently, the high point of the meal was looking to be a sweet corn and lima bean succotash.

He sighed. "Go ahead and get me the phone, Bug. The magnet, too." It was a testament to either his optimism or his blind stubbornness that he didn't just program the pizza place's number into the house phone. Grabbing his own wineglass, he asked Shay, "What do you like on your pizza?"

SHAY WHISTLED. "Well, this is impressive."

Holding the woman's hand as they surveyed the table together, Vicki nodded happily. "Daddy does dessert good. And dessert's the most important part!"

Mark rocked back on his heels, glad he'd succeeded in this at least. Not that dinner had been a total disaster. He'd had a blast, not just talking to Shay, which he always enjoyed, but watching her interact with his daughter. After pizza, he'd sent the girls into the living room while he cleared away the cardboard boxes and dishes. Vicki had reenacted the ballet routine from her holiday minirecital and given Shay a preview of April's big number.

Meanwhile, Mark had pulled out a carton of strawberries he'd washed earlier in the day, sliced some bananas, tore half of an angel food cake into bite-size chunks and dumped a bag of large marshmallows into a heart-shaped bowl. Finally, he'd set up a top-of-the-line camping stove—one that was ultra clean burning and safer than propane—on the table to heat chocolate.

"Chocolate fondue," he said. He handed each female a skewer and winked at Shay. "We're very fancy here."

"Well, duh. Hence the headgear." She pointed at the tiara she now wore. When she'd told Vicki during dinner how much she liked the flashy Valentine headband, Vicki had decided their guest needed something equally dazzling. So the principal of Woodside sat at his kitchen table in her stocking feet and a glittering rhinestone crown.

They ate with enthusiasm and when Mark once again refused to let his date help clean the kitchen, Shay instead offered to help Vicki get ready for bed.

"Do I hafta?" The little girl made a face, even though Mark knew that after the way she'd been racing around all night to show off her every favorite book, toy and stuffed animal, she'd probably be asleep in minutes.

Before Mark could even answer, Shay straightened in her chair, adopting the same tone he imagined she used when admonishing students not to run in the halls or to use their indoor voices in the lunchroom. "Well, it is a school night, young lady."

"Okay." Vicki heaved a sigh, then brightened, finding the silver lining. "Least I don't hafta clean up. We got chocolate everywhere."

Mark laughed. *"We?"*

His daughter sent him a sheepish look from beneath her lashes. "Sorry."

"I was going to get a couple of logs out of the garage for the fireplace," Mark told Shay. "Want me to make some coffee, too?"

"Sounds nice," she agreed, her slow smile making his heart thump double-time against his ribs.

It *was* a school night, but, much to his pleasure, Shay didn't seem to be in a hurry to leave. As much as Mark had enjoyed watching his daughter interact with their guest, he was looking forward to being alone with Shay.

Vicki climbed down from her chair and held her hand out to Shay. "Wanna help me pick out my pj's?"

"Hmm…what say we wash those hands first, sticky fingers?" Shay went to the sink and gave Vicki the liquid soap that was tough to reach.

"Daddy says I'm not supposed to tell anyone at school

about this," Vicki announced as she rubbed her fingers together beneath the stream of water.

"He did?" Shay looked unsure what to do with this news.

"It's okay," Vicki said. "It's like a secret. A good secret. But I can still hug you at school, right?"

"Always." As if to prove her point, Shay swept the little girl into her arms. Vicki's hands were clean, but her face was another story. Shay swiped a damp paper towel over her face. "There, beautiful again. Don't you think so, Daddy?" She angled her body so that she was holding Vicki toward him.

Mark's throat closed, emotion making it impossible to breathe. The sight of his daughter, balanced on Shay's hip and snuggled against her, was wrenchingly poignant. It should have been comical, those sparkly red hearts sticking out of Vicki's mass of curls and Shay standing there with a too-small tiara perched on her head.

I could love this woman.

"Daddy?" Vicki seemed piqued that he'd yet to validate her fresh-faced gorgeousness. "You look funny."

"Don't worry," he said absently. "I'm all right."

And he was, he realized. He'd had one of those moments of nearly paralyzing awe—like a time he'd seen a perfect rainbow fill the entire sky or went jogging in the woods and came within inches of a doe and her fawn. But the emotion welling in him wasn't sadness. Or fear. Or guilt. He'd come face-to-face with just how deep his feelings ran for Shay—how deep they could become— and his response was sheer joy. Mixed in with a touch of old-fashioned nerves.

Dee, Cade, Vicki—they'd all asked variations of the same question, wanting to know if he thought he would ever be part of a serious relationship again. And he'd demurred with "maybe," "someday," or a plain, "I don't know." For the first time, his answer, even if no one else got to hear it, was *God, I hope so.*

SHAY STOOD IN THE DOORWAY watching as Mark tucked in his daughter. He kissed Vicki's cheek and wished her sweet dreams.

"Pinky, too," she mumbled drowsily, proffering a stuffed pony.

Mark obligingly kissed the pony on the white blaze that ran down its face, then turned to leave.

"Wait." Vicki propped herself up on her elbows, but it wasn't her father she was addressing. "Principal Morgan, do I have to still call you Principal Morgan?"

Shay hadn't been expecting the question. "What did you want to call me?"

"Ms. Shay? Like I do with Ms. Charlotte and our other friends?"

"All right, but not at school. At school, I'm still Principal Morgan. You can call me Shay other times, like tonight."

"Does that mean you're coming back to our house?" Vicki asked shrewdly.

Shay exchanged glances with Mark, thought about what a change it was from spending a quiet evening alone to laughing through three hours with the two of them. Eating together and teasing each other and feeling even the tiniest bit maternal as she'd given Vicki a pep talk about overcoming stage fright for her big ballet recital and wiped smudges of chocolate off the girl's face. "Um, yeah, I guess I am…if that's okay with you and your dad."

In response, Vicki beamed a smile brighter than her night-light.

For over a week, Shay had been looking forward to kissing Mark again, but once they were back in the living room, with only the crackling fire for company, she felt unaccountably shy. She sipped the last of her merlot, wondering if the effects of their last kiss had been magnified because it was their first, because she hadn't expected it. Would he once again cause her toes to curl, make her body melt with sensual need?

He sat next to her on the couch, placing his arm on the backrest but not quite touching her. "Coffee's brewing. Hope you weren't in a hurry?"

She shook her head, humming a few notes of an old song, "Baby, It's Cold Outside." How could driving home in the snow possibly compare to sharing a glass of rich, mellow wine with an incredibly good-looking guy who'd just cooked for her. Well, sort of.

She grinned, angling toward him, resting her head against his arm. "Dinner was—"

"Let's never speak of it."

"All right, then. Can I at least tell you that dessert was spectacular? I've always had a raging sweet tooth."

"Good to know for gift-giving occasions." He, too, had leaned in, his head close to hers. "When's your birthday? I seem to recall you mentioning that we were both Aries. At the hospital? Or did I imagine that after they pumped me full of painkiller?"

"March 29. My mom's got a family dinner all planned." And wouldn't Pamela Morgan do cartwheels of joy if her daughter invited Mark and his adorable daughter? "Does Vicki have any grandparents living?" She'd only really heard Mark mention Vicki's aunt.

"No. Jess and Dee lost their parents in a car crash the first year we were married. Neither of them got to see Vicki born. My dad died the week before we learned Jess was pregnant." It had been such a bittersweet time for the family. "Victor Hathaway. Vicki's named for him. Mom moved into the Braeden assisted-living senior community and died a couple of years later, in her sleep. She used to love when we brought—" He straightened suddenly. "You gave me a great idea."

"Happy to help," Shay said, baffled. She had no idea what he was talking about.

"I should call the senior community director, see if the Campside Girls could come sing or even play Uno. A lot of the residents are healthy and active, they're just lonely." He sobered, looking as if he had firsthand sympathy with their plight. "A visit from some cheerful little girls might be a real day brightener. And it might also be nice for kids like Vicki who don't have grandparents, or at least not near enough to visit on a regular basis."

"Careful," Shay teased. "Vicki might post a notice at the home soliciting grandparents."

"Her latest is that she wants a sister."

"Oh." Shay wasn't sure what to say to that. Technically, Vicki's dreams for the future had nothing to do with her, yet...

"You have that nervous look again," Mark observed. "The same one you had when Vicki asked if she still has to call you Principal Morgan. Were you afraid she was going to ask if she could start calling you mom?"

"It crossed my mind," Shay admitted. "Is it all right that I told her I'd be coming back? Maybe I was overstepping with that assumption."

He tried to take both her hands in his, the action

slightly hampered by the wrist-to-fingertip brace he still wore. "Come back as often as you like. We want you here." He gave her a crooked grin that managed to be both boyish and sexy. "Especially me."

Shay leaned forward, kissing him gently. It wasn't the brazen, all-out carnal assault of last time. But the softer slow burn was just as effective. He ran his good hand lightly up her back, causing shivers of sensation along her spine. He nipped at her lower lip and drew it between his own, kissing her lazily. Thoroughly. She felt like she was the chocolate fondue, her insides pooling into something warm and sweet. It was very arousing to be in the arms of a man who seemed so willing to take his time.

She grinned against his lips. "You taste like red wine."

"Is that a problem?" he asked. He moved away from her mouth, trailing kisses up the side of her neck.

"No, it's just…mmm." She closed her eyes, tilting her head and allowing him better access. "In my mind, you'll always taste like peppermint. Like the first time you kissed me."

He angled back just long enough to meet her eyes. "I think I have some peppermints around here if you want to re-create the moment."

She pulled him to her. "You're doing just fine without them."

SHAY'S HIGH-HEELED SHOES clicked loudly on the hard floor, echoing through the fourth-grade hall, but she felt as if she were walking on clouds as she returned to her office. It had been late when she'd left Mark's last night—they'd necked in front of his fireplace for hours like a couple of teenagers, then he'd insisted on taking the keys to her car and warming it up for her. He'd also insisted she text him when she got home so that he'd know she'd arrived safely. She'd worried on the drive that she might be sluggish and groggy today.

Quite the contrary.

She'd rolled out of bed with a smile on her face, so enchanted with the world that she'd stopped on her way to the school to buy a couple of doughnuts for Roberta. The secretary had regarded the white bakery bag suspiciously, as if she expected ticking from within, but she'd forced herself to say thank you. Even slow progress was progress.

As she reentered the administrative office suite, she made a point of smiling at the secretary.

Roberta pointed to the row of visitor chairs against the wall. "Mrs. Dubois to see you."

Shay sighed inwardly. Kate Dubois was early. But no matter. Shay knew what the woman wanted and already knew how this meeting would go—might as well get it over with. "Good morning, Mrs. Dubois. If you'll follow me, please?"

The woman nodded tersely and stood, carrying with her a large manila folder so full that papers were spilling out. Shay picked up a piece of paper printed with testing scores and handed it back. No doubt all the documents in the folder were evidence of Stefan Dubois's six-year-old genius. Shay had seen his grades and testing scores; they did nothing to reverse budget cuts and district policy.

Furthermore, Shay had already followed up on Mrs. Dubois's earlier request by talking to the Gifted Arts teacher, Elsie Jenkins.

"Stefan's a bright kid, no question about it," Elsie had

agreed. "He remembers everything you teach him and is probably going to be an honors student when he gets to middle school years from now. But…he doesn't show much creativity or outside-the-box thinking when asked to solve problems. We don't just look at test scores when we evaluate for the gifted program, not that it matters yet."

Inside Shay's office, she indicated the small table and shut the door behind them.

Kate wasted no time, launching straight into her complaint. "My Stefan is an exemplary student—"

"He absolutely is," Shay interrupted, aiming to surprise the other woman with her quick agreement and perhaps take some of the wind out of her maternal sails. "Mrs. Frost is very proud of him and says he's a courteous student."

"Yes, well." Kate fidgeted with the bright orange scarf she wore, looking slightly mollified. "And does Mrs. Frost think that he belongs in the gifted program? His brother Samuel has been in Gifted Arts here at Woodside for the past three years and we were quite distressed to learn Stefan would not be getting that opportunity."

"He may well get it," Shay pointed out. "In third grade. As you're probably aware, the district has made some significant cuts. Resources for the Gifted Arts program have been further limited, making it possible for us to offer the program only to our third through fifth graders."

Kate leaned forward in her chair, eyes glinting. "This is not my first rodeo, Ms. Morgan. Stefan is the youngest of four, and we've been in this school district a lot longer than you have. I know that the fine print of many policies is that principals of individual schools have some discretion as to how the policies are implemented. You could find a way to make an exception."

And get lynched by the other parents? No, thank you. Shay could have explained that, even if she was inclined to make exceptions, Mrs. Jenkins didn't think Stefan was a good candidate for Gifted Arts—but that felt too much like throwing one of her teachers under the bus.

She gave the woman a thin smile. "Mrs. Dubois, I'm flattered, but I think you overestimate my godlike power. I can't just overturn policies willy-nilly for one student. My door is always open to parents, but I'm afraid this particular subject is closed."

Kate was so visibly angry her nostrils were flaring. But she didn't seem to know what else to say to press her case. So she stood. "I will be writing to the school board about this."

"Best of luck," Shay said. "I for one would love to see some of the financial resources reallocated to the program."

The woman paused, her hand on the door. "Can't help but wonder if you would have made an exception for Victoria Hathaway."

"Excuse me?"

Kate looked back over her shoulder, her expression an ill-concealed sneer. "Carolyn mentioned how you and Mark Hathaway went to the town meeting together. And dinner afterward. And the roller-skating rink. Interesting how no first graders were book buddies until Victoria."

Shay gripped the edge of the table so tightly she expected to hear the wood splinter. "If Stefan is interested in reading to the kindergarten classes, I'm certain I can arrange it. That doesn't require extra funding or faculty, after all. As to anything else…I do not discuss one student or their family with another student's family. I want everyone who comes into this office to be assured of the confidentiality of whatever they say. Good day, Mrs. Dubois."

At least, it *had* been.

Chapter Twelve

The Monday evening after Valentine's Day was the first official Campside Girls meeting at Woodside. Mark certainly had plenty to think about in terms of getting the girls organized and keeping them on track as they attempted a craft project Dee had explained to him via email. "These are easy to follow step-by-step instructions," she'd promised. Yeah, but so were most recipes, had been his skeptical response. He also wanted to start working with the girls on some songs that they could perform at the Braeden senior community next month—he'd called the director last Friday and she'd been thrilled by the idea.

Yet all thoughts of Campside Girls activities temporarily fled when he pulled into the school parking lot and saw Shay's car still there. She must be working late. His body temperature shot up at least five degrees at the prospect of seeing her. She'd called him several times since Valentine's Day and they'd had many wonderful conversations. She certainly didn't seem to regret the hours they'd spent in front of his fireplace last week. Yet she'd turned down both his invitations for lunch during the school week and his offer to join him and Vicki for a movie. He'd even said that Dee might be willing to babysit if Shay would rather do something just as adults. He hadn't yet told Dee about his budding relationship, finding himself oddly protective of it and not wanting to share it with outsiders, but he would without question if it meant getting to spend more time with Shay.

Was he being paranoid or had she subtly retreated?

He had arrived early, wanting to be the first person at the meeting so he could set up everything. Vicki had ridden the bus home with Tessa today and Charlotte was bringing both of the girls later. He had a few minutes to stop by her office, if Shay wasn't in a meeting or otherwise critically occupied.

The school secretary appeared to have gone home already but the door to the front office was open.

"Hello?" he called out. It was surreal to be here when it was so quiet. An elementary school without children's voices was like an amusement park with no rides.

There was rustling from down the hall. "Mark, is that you?" And then, just as she had the first day he'd met her, Shay poked her head out of the principal's office. But this time, his heart raced wildly at the sight of her. She'd kicked off her shoes and her hair was loose around her face. She was wearing a cranberry-colored sweaterdress that reminded him of the red wine they'd shared last time he saw her.

"Hi," he said softly.

Her eyes had widened in greeting, her mouth curving into a sweet smile. But when he spoke, it was as if he'd broken a spell. She literally took a step back, even though yards of carpet separated them, and her expression became one of professional civility rather than uncensored happiness to see him.

"Good to see you," she said crisply. "I'd almost

forgotten that tonight was our first Campside Girls meeting. Need any help with that?" she asked, nodding to the cardboard box balanced in his arms and the plastic bag looped over one forearm.

"That would be great," he said. "If I'm not taking you away from anything?" Of course he was. Why else would she be here so late?

"Just let me slide my shoes back on." She ducked into her office, then returned, an inch and a half taller. "You should let me take the box."

"That goes against my manly instincts," he complained.

She rolled her eyes. "Surely you don't plan to teach the girls in your troop that they're weak and need big strong guys to do things for them?"

Sheesh, when she put it like *that*. He handed over the box, waiting a beat before he asked, "Isn't it all right if I occasionally do things for a strong, savvy woman to show her how much she's appreciated?"

Her grin was irrepressible, making her once again look like herself—the woman who'd worn a tiara in his kitchen and kissed him back so ardently—instead of a polite but distant school administrator who barely knew him. "I suppose that would be all right."

They walked down the hall together. Since he didn't see or hear anyone else, he quietly voiced the question that had been plaguing him for a week, "Shay, are you avoiding me?"

Her footsteps faltered, but she kept her head high, her gaze straight ahead. "I just volunteered to walk with you to the cafeteria. Avoiding would have been if I'd hid out at my desk and pretended not to hear you come in."

"I meant avoiding in the personal sense."

She still hadn't looked at him but now a light stain of color was climbing her cheeks.

"I knew it!" What he didn't know was why. "Did I do something to upset you?"

"Look, I've been busy, okay? Don't automatically assume it's about you," she cautioned gently. Even though there was no real sting in her tone, he flinched, feeling like an obsessive egomaniac. "I've just had a lot on my plate, including alienating community leaders."

"What do you mean?" He asked more for her than himself. She sounded distressed and he wanted to help if he could.

She led the way into the empty cafeteria and set the box down on the nearest table. Then she propped her hip against it, shoving a hand through her hair. Golden waves spilled over her fingers. "I was approached by a woman this morning who wants a booth at our fair. The official process is to go through the PTA president and then she brings all requests to me to rubber-stamp. Of course, not everyone has done it that way."

Him, for instance. Because he'd already spoken to Ridenour in the fall, it had never occurred to him not to ask Shay directly about the Fitness Fair. Had it been an abuse of their relationship, framing the request casually instead of using the proper channels?

She waved a hand. "I suppose it doesn't matter, since they all come to me eventually anyway, but it helps me build a healthy relationship with the PTA officers when I respect procedure. I'm doing a lot of committee work with them right now to try and establish that we're a team, all on the same side."

"So do you think you're 'alienating' people because this woman went around the PTA?"

"No. Because I told her no…and she's married to one of the town councilmen. A fact she mentioned repeatedly in our fifteen-minute meeting."

Shay shook her head, looking disgusted. "I didn't even want to give her an answer. I encouraged her to submit her information, either by leaving some with me or giving it to Nancy, our president, and promised someone would get back to her. But she insisted on a decision. She's a sales representative for an herbal pharmaceuticals company. None of her products are safe for kids—I'm not entirely convinced they're all safe for adults—so I didn't think an elementary school fair would be the appropriate venue. I don't want to be accused of sending our students the wrong message."

"And she didn't understand that?" Mark asked, leaning against the table next to her.

"You know what she told me?" Shay adopted a thick accent and mimicked the voice so well that Mark knew exactly which councilman's wife she meant—an opinionated size two he'd never particularly liked. "'Sugar, the pills aren't for the kids, they're for the mothers. Honestly, have you *seen* some of those women?'"

Mark laughed. He didn't mean to, but he couldn't stop himself. "Has anyone ever told you that you do a wicked impression, Principal Morgan?"

She flashed him a smile. "I am a woman of many talents."

"I'm sorry you had a difficult day." He stood, relieved that she wasn't looking quite so tense anymore, and began pulling supplies out of the box. Although he'd had a few minutes to spare when he first entered the building, if he didn't get his butt in gear, he'd find himself running late. "Did I tell you the good news? Two moms and one of your science teachers have volunteered to help with the camping trip, so we're a go!"

Shay wrinkled her nose. "I have to say, the whole appeal of sleeping on the ground and slathering myself under an inch of bug spray is still lost on me. But if anything was going to make me a believer, it would be the discovery that you can make really scrumptious dessert with camping stoves."

He laughed. "I'll make sure to bring plenty of chocolate for the girls in case some of them find themselves sharing your opinion."

"Mark? Before the girls come, there's something I want to get off my chest."

He stilled, her tone not boding well. "All right."

"There's no district policy that, uh, forbids someone in my position from 'fraternizing' with a parent. We're not doing anything wrong. But I hate that when that woman stormed out of my office today, I had to consider that she could complain I told her no while I said yes to my...well, to you."

"You don't really think anyone would take a trumped-up grievance like that seriously?" Mark didn't mean to belittle her concerns, but surely people were more reasonable than that.

Weren't they?

"A similar insinuation was already made," she said. "A mother implied I gave Vicki special treatment because she's your daughter. It's stupid—I know that and most people would probably see it. But...I really want to do a good job here. I've waited a long time for this opportunity."

"And I'm jeopardizing that?" he asked tightly.

"I don't know. Probably not?" She sounded completely

unconvinced of her own statement. "Can I just have some space? To think it all over?"

"Sure." The word felt barbed in his throat, as if it cut into him to say.

"Thank you." She rose on her tiptoes to press a furtive kiss against his cheek before hurrying toward the double doors. "I appreciate your being understanding."

Like he had a choice? Mark hadn't dated much, but he figured enlightened men respected a woman's emotional needs. Even though what he really wanted to do was throw something at the far wall.

In the Campside Girls handbook, it said learning new vocabulary could help them earn the Adventures in Literacy badge, but Mark doubted that the words he was biting back now were what the CG founders had in mind.

"WHOA!" GENEVA DUCKED out of the way, then reached for the remote. "You want to tell me what gives, Sugar Ray Shay? That's the second close call in the last fifteen minutes."

"Sorry," Shay said breathlessly. "My jab got away from me." Kickboxing in an enclosed space was not without its dangers.

Geneva had stopped the DVD while Shay apologized. "We're done for the time being. You have some serious aggression going on. Is this still about that woman yesterday who wanted to peddle diet pills to students and their allegedly fat mamas?"

When Shay had arrived this evening, she'd told that story. Even though the woman in question didn't have a child at the school—meaning Shay wasn't obligated to keep a parent, teacher or student confidence—she'd spoken in generalities rather than naming names. Nonetheless, Geneva had immediately guessed who the culprit was and declared her "a pain in the butt from way back."

"It's not that." Shay reached for a bottle of water, trying to find a way to articulate what was bothering her without sounding like a coward, overly intimidated by what people thought of her. Or worse, a heartless wretch who cared more about climbing the career ladder than about people.

The truth was, there were a lot of ways she could help this school and the people in it. She'd implemented some mentoring programs, was working alongside a proud special ed teacher to help a student with Asperger's make the leap into an inclusion classroom next year, had been making plans with the media center specialist to get Woodside involved in a county reading bowl for the first time. She'd also been busting her tail to secure more money for the art and music departments, which would benefit every child at Woodside.

But she couldn't do any of those things if she lost this job to a "permanent" replacement by next fall. So, while she wasn't the type to let other people's opinions define her, she recognized that now was probably not a prudent time to antagonize people apt to fire off angry letters to the school board.

Shay sat on an exercise mat, leaning against the wall. "I'm upset about Mark."

"*Why?* From everything you've told me, he sounds darn near perfect. Nothing a few cooking lessons couldn't cure. I can't believe I'm the one who got dumped, and you're the one who's so cranky."

Shay rolled her eyes. "Cade didn't 'dump' you. At least, not in the version you told me earlier."

He'd left town for a few days to deliver some custom-made furniture to someone in another state and mentioned that he'd been invited to visit an old friend on the way back. A female friend. Sensing the question he'd been dancing around, Geneva had assured him that he was not answerable to her. Besides, as much fun as she'd had with him for the past month, she didn't see any real future with someone who hated her favorite book of all time. *And how can he even have an informed opinion,* Geneva had asked, *when he never made it past chapter three?*

"I was just trying to make a point," Geneva admitted, plopping down on the exercise ball Shay had given her, rolling it back and forth while she talked. "I always knew that Cade and I had an expiration date. He was a blast, but he wasn't…special. We weren't special to each other, rather. You know? But I get the impression that you and Mark are."

Shay gnawed at her lower lip, a bad habit from adolescence. In high school, if she was worried about an exam, she'd have her lipstick completely chewed off by homeroom. "He's special. But he's also got horrible timing." The question of her job aside, there was *his* to worry about. Even though she couldn't tell Geneva, there was a possibility Mark might be leaving Braeden by summer.

His weeklong sales event had gone well and he reported that the Bullards, the couple who won the free night at Hawk Summit, were headed there soon and had actually booked two additional paid nights. At the next town council meeting, they were voting on the official reopening of the Douglas Lodge. But these were seeds being planted for future growth, not dramatic, immediate solutions.

And if one or both of you leave Braeden, are you going to be content to say goodbye without regrets...or are you going to wish you'd made the most of the time you'd had together?

"Shay, guys like Mark don't come along that often, and if you don't want him, some other lucky woman is going to snap him up. But if you do want him..."

"I do." The words were so easy to say, to admit to herself. So why was she here sweating in Geneva's basement when she could be making the most of her potentially limited time with the best guy she'd ever met?

HAVING TUCKED VICKI IN for bed, Mark had just stretched out on the couch to catch part of a basketball game when his cell phone chirped, signaling a text message. He picked it up off the coffee table, surprised to see Shay's name on the screen.

You awake?

He laughed. Granted, his social life hadn't been a frenzy of wild and crazy parties for the past few years, but he wasn't such a stick-in-the-mud that he was asleep this early.

Yep.

He held his breath waiting for his response. Yesterday, she'd asked for space. Did her contacting him mean she'd changed her mind? He tried to tamp down his rising hopes in case her texting was for something as mundane as a question about the Campside Girls or telling Mark she'd dropped an earring at his house last week.

Been thinking. Offer still good of getting Dee to babysit?

So that they could go out? His heart was thundering as he responded.

Good on my end, have to confirm with her. Want me to call you after?

An eternity passed in the second it took her to type: Yes.

Okay. Talk soon.

"Yes!" He wasn't entirely sure what had changed Shay's mind, nor was he sure he cared. He muted the basketball game then, with fingers that shook, dialed his sister-in-law's phone number. "Dee? It's Mark."

"Hey, stranger. I feel like we haven't seen you enough lately. Sorry we had to cancel the weekly dinner tonight."

"Don't be silly. It's great that Bobby's in a chess tournament. How'd he do?"

They chatted for a few minutes about his nephew and about his first Campside Girls meeting and his enthusiasm for the upcoming campout and singing for the seniors. It had seemed rude to launch into asking her for a favor as soon as she picked up the phone, but Mark couldn't wait any longer.

"Dee, you know how you've always said you'd be willing to watch Vicki if I…wanted an adult night out?"

His sister-in-law actually squealed. "You're going to ask the principal on a date, aren't you? Oh, Mark, that's fantastic."

"How did you know it was Shay?" he asked, omitting mention of the fact that he'd already asked her.

"Um…I don't want to make you feel self-conscious, but there have been a few harmless rumors."

He let his head fall back against the couch's armrest. "Wonderful." No doubt that "harmless" gossip was fueling her reticence to see him. "I'm more worried about her feeling self-conscious, so if you could keep this to yourself?"

"Got it. On the down low, my lips are sealed, it's in the vault!"

For his sister-in-law to be prattling nonsensically, she must be really happy for him. "Thank you, Dee. So any chance you're available one night this weekend?"

"Friday works for me if it works for you and Shay. Tell you what, you can have Vicki pack an overnight bag. You know, just let her fall asleep in one place and stay put instead of having to move her or wake her up if the two of you are…out late."

At the thought of an entire night with Shay, he almost had to put his head between his knees to force blood back to his brain. But having this conversation with Dee was incredibly awkward, so he cleared his throat, informed her, "I'll get back you on that" and hung up the phone.

He took several deep breaths before punching in Shay's number and worked hard not to sound like an overeager fourteen-year-old when she answered.

"How does Friday sound to you?" he asked. "We could do dinner or a movie. Or both, actually. Dee said she would just let Vicki spend the night if we'd like to stay out late."

Shay digested this information. "Or," she said slowly, "we could get takeout and rent something and have dinner and a movie at my place."

Because she'd rather not run into anyone affiliated with the school or because she wanted to be alone with him as badly as he did with her? Choosing to believe it was the latter, he told her, "It's a date."

"You look beautiful," Mark said once Shay had opened the door. "No surprise there, though. You always look beautiful to me."

She laughed. "That's because you haven't seen me sweaty and disheveled in my ratty workout clothes."

Would he sound disturbed if he told her he was pretty sure he'd think she was gorgeous even then? Keeping that opinion to himself, he handed her a small bouquet of white and blue flowers. Roses probably would have been more romantic, but the blue had made him think of her eyes.

"Thank you." She led him inside, smoothing a hand over her denim skirt. She'd paired it with a loose, scoop-neck violet sweater. Shay had mentioned once that she enjoyed playing Scrabble—with that neckline, she could beat him even if her only letters were a *Q* and six *E*s. "Can I let you in on a secret?"

"Please." He shrugged out of his jacket. Lord, it was warm in here.

She grinned. "I changed clothes four times. Everything either seemed too dressy for an evening at home or so casual that it looked like I didn't care. But I do."

He reached out, running his fingers through her hair and cupping the back of her neck. "Thank you for giving this a chance." Bending down, he kissed her hello.

It was a far superior custom than kissing someone good-night, knowing that your time with them had passed too quickly. This way, the entire night stretched ahead of them, the possibilities dizzying.

Shay broke away from the kiss only for a moment. "Your hand! It's not wrapped anymore."

"Went to the doctor today. I'm a whole man again." Even though he was joking, truer words had never been spoken. He *did* feel whole. And alive. And excited. For too many months, he'd been going through motions— caring, perhaps, especially about his daughter, but not really trying. Now, he and Vicki were closer than they'd ever been. And while the store was struggling, he was excited by the challenge and invigorated by ideas. He was glad he'd signed on to be a troop leader.

But he was especially glad for this woman in his arms and the way she'd changed not only his life but him.

He pulled her tighter against him. "You are amazing. You know that?"

She looked surprised but delighted by this declaration. "Yes, but pretend I don't know and tell me anyway."

It was odd to be chuckling and kissing at the same time, but not unpleasant. She opened her mouth against his, letting him in, and as their tongues met and their bodies pressed closer together, the laughter faded, leaving something hotter and more intense in its wake. Distantly, Mark heard the flowers she dropped hit the floor. He felt Shay's hands on his body, one on his neck and one fisted in the back of his shirt as if part of her wanted to tear his clothes off. Desire roared through him. He wanted to be touched everywhere, was hungry to touch her.

It was the soft, urgent noises she made in the back of her throat that sent him over the edge. He scooped her up in his arms. "Bedroom?" It was both a plea for permission and a request for directions.

She nodded, her eyes glazed and her lips swollen, pointing the way.

As it turned out, they never did watch their intended movie. And they didn't get around to reheating dinner until hours later.

Chapter Thirteen

"No, I see what you mean," Mark agreed, leaning back in his desk chair. It was the last week in March—over the past month, he and Jeffrey from Hawk Summit had struck up not only an informal professional alliance but a legitimate friendship. So when Jeffrey had called that morning to ask if he could send over a press release he wasn't entirely pleased with, Mark had said of course. "It definitely misses some of the points you wanted to make.

"Tell you what," Mark continued. "I have a couple of suggestions I'll email back to you."

"I appreciate that. It's damn frustrating paying PR consultants for work that I—or someone else—ends up having to fix," Jeffrey grumbled. "When are you going to take me up on my offer?"

As his way of saying thanks for Mark's promotional efforts on behalf of the ski resort, Jeffrey kept inviting Mark to bring Shay up some weekend at a deeply discounted price. It was a very tempting idea. Then again, the idea of being alone with her anywhere sounded good.

Mark adored his daughter, and Shay was fantastic with Vicki, but it was difficult to find quality alone time with your lover when you were trying to set a good example for a child. The only time Mark and Shay got to have a sleepover was when Vicki had one elsewhere, and since he didn't want his daughter to think he was trying to get rid of her all the time, he—

"You still there?" Jeffrey asked, sounding amused.

"Yeah." Mark cleared his throat. "Sorry. Guess I got distracted."

Jeffrey laughed. "I really want to meet this gal some-day."

"You will, but this weekend, I am off to take eight little girls camping. Oh, and word of advice? When you do meet Shay, I wouldn't call her a 'gal.'"

A buzzing came from among the papers on Mark's desk, and he frowned, expecting to find some kind of large bug. It took him a second to realize that his cell phone, set to vibrate, was vying for his attention.

"Jeff, are we all done? Someone else is trying to catch me on my other phone."

"No prob. Thanks again," Jeffrey said right before he disconnected.

Mark simultaneously hung up his office phone and fished out the cell. "Hello?"

"Mark, it's Susan." Susan Webb was the science teacher from Woodside who'd agreed to act as the third necessary chaperone for this trip. He could run a meeting in the cafeteria alone if he absolutely had to, but Campside Girls took their liability very seriously. For overnight trips out into the woods at this age level, there was a one adult per two children ratio.

As a bonus, because Susan was a science teacher, she'd planned a couple of fun experiments as well as stargazing Saturday night that would help them earn a junior astronomy badge.

"Bad news," she said, sounding shaky. "I threw up about half an hour ago. Left the school, I'm at home now."

But what about the campout? Mark pulled together just enough shreds of chivalry and plain human decency not to blurt the selfish question. "That's awful." *On multiple levels.* "I hope you feel better soon."

"Obviously this means I can't— Gotta go!"

The phone went dead and Mark stared at the cell in his hand. Poor Susan.

All right, this was a setback, but they didn't leave for the campground until after school let out for the day. He still had a few hours to find a replacement. He didn't even bother calling Charlotte Wilkes—he knew the reason she hadn't volunteered to come with Tessa in the first place was because she had something going on with her older daughter this weekend. So he tried another mom on the troop phone tree list and left a message. He'd call a few more and if nothing else, grovel to his sister-in-law, even though she didn't have a daughter and had never actually been a Campside Girl herself.

"Hey, boss?" Roddy's deep voice came down the hall. "Someone up front to see you."

Mark tossed his phone back onto the desk, deciding it would be grossly unprofessional to make calls while helping a customer. Although clearly that philosophy didn't extend both ways—more than once he'd been summoned to assist someone who continued carrying on a conversation. The worst were the customers with earpieces who wandered the store like crazy people muttering to—and occasionally arguing with—themselves.

Before Mark even made it out of the back hallway, his visitor appeared, wringing a grin from him despite the unfortunate news he'd just been given.

"Shay! What are you doing here?"

"I am occasionally allowed to leave my office for lunch." She came to him with an enthusiastic kiss that made all his troubles recede. Though it was hardly a secret in town that they were dating—it had been a month, after all, and Braeden wasn't that big—she was still hesitant to make big public displays of affection. He savored stolen moments like these.

"I was just talking about you a few minutes ago," Mark told her, smoothing her hair away from her face. Her hair was already perfect, but he liked the excuse to touch her. "I was on the phone with Jeffrey again and he wants to meet you. Probably thinks you're a figment of my imagination."

"Maybe we could skip the birthday meal with my family next week and go meet Jeffrey instead," she offered, her eyes twinkling.

He laughed. "I'm looking forward to meeting your parents."

"My mother is going to insist you call her Mom and my father will probably excuse himself between dinner and dessert to do a criminal background check on you. And the fuss they're going to make over Vicki is probably going to freak her out."

"It will be fine," he promised. "You want to wait here while I get my wallet and cell phone and I'll take you out to lunch?"

She shook her head. "Actually, I was hoping you'd take a few minutes to help me in the store." She contorted her face into an exaggerated grimace. "I need to purchase a sleeping bag. I hear you need one if you're going camping."

"*You're* going camping? Wait, does this—"

"You forget, Susan Webb is one of my faculty. I knew she was sick before you did, and I've decided to offer my services this weekend. I'm even a former science teacher. Unless," she added somewhat shyly, "you've already found a replacement?"

"No." Mark pumped a fist in the air. "This is fantastic! But are you sure? You've never made any secret of the fact that you consider roughing it a place where they don't leave mints on the pillows."

"Well, you are having dinner with my family Tuesday, so I owe you."

"Meeting your family is not a hardship," he reminded her for the umpteenth time.

"You say that because you haven't met them," she warned. "Come on, let's go spend obscene chunks of my salary on camping gear so you can demonstrate to your boss what a charming and effective salesman you are."

"This is going to be great," he told her. "You're going to love camping." He and Shay, together beneath a canopy of stars? The only thing that could possibly make it more perfect was if they were allowed to sleep in the same tent and didn't have eight juvenile witnesses. Other than that, it fit his idea of paradise to a T.

THIS WAS TURNING INTO the longest weekend of Mark's life—and they hadn't even made it to Friday night yet.

Trying to get the girls sorted in the school parking lot into two groups of four had been chaotic enough. The plan was that he and Shay would take one group of four in Dee's borrowed van, and the two volunteer moms, Julie and Kris, would take the other four in Julie's SUV. As if it weren't bad enough that Mark had to contend with eight first- and second-grade girls arguing about who got to sit next to whom and which one was the "cool" car, he'd noticed Shay's face flame when Julie whispered just a little too loudly to Kris, "I didn't know we were allowed to bring dates on this trip."

He'd assumed the trip would smooth out once they were on the road, but that was before Julie blew a tire, not to mention two separate potty stops in the last hour and a piercing shriek worthy of a wailing banshee that nearly sent him off the road. Apparently someone had told six-year-old Meghan that there were poisonous snakes living at the campground and that one would probably bite her in her sleep. After her initial screech, she'd burst into tears and was now hysterically sobbing, *"Take me back, Mr. Mark, take me back!"*

Shay leaned close to him, her voice a whisper—not that any of the kids in the backseat could have heard her over Meghan anyway. "Are we having fun yet? Hey, girls, who wants to hear something weird about snakes?"

She got a chorus of "me!" from three of them and a cautious sniffle from Meghan. For the next twenty minutes, Shay shared with them all sorts of strange trivia about different wildlife, from funny stories she swore were true to the kind of "eww, gross" anecdotes that made children giggle. Mark would have thrown his arms around her in gratitude if he weren't busy steering.

When they finally reached the campsite the girls spilled out of the van, all talking at once, to greet the other four as if they hadn't seen them in a month of Sundays—and hadn't all been arguing at the start of the trip. Mark took just a second to breathe deeply before he joined his charges.

"You were great with them," he told Shay.

She paused, her fingers wrapped around the door handle, and teased, "Yeah. I should probably find some kind of job working with kids, don't you think?"

"Smart-ass," he said affectionately. "But I'm too grateful to care. You can have anything you want for your birthday. Just name it, and I promise you'll get it."

"That shouldn't be too difficult a promise to keep." Slowly she let her gaze drop down over him in suggestive perusal. "I know exactly what I want."

He grinned. "May I say, you have excellent taste."

EVEN THOUGH THERE WERE a few snags, the weekend was deemed a success. The nights were too cloudy for stargazing, but the chilly, overcast weather meant that there were no mosquitoes to bother anyone. It was easy enough for the girls to stay warm by putting on coats, huddling into fleecy sleeping bags or roasting marsh-mallows around the small fire. Shay headed up a nature hike, pointing out different kinds of plants and animals, and Meghan redeemed herself when a lizard crawled onto her arm and she thought it was "cute."

One of the oldest girls in the troop, a second grader who'd already had her eighth birthday, shrieked when Meghan turned to show off her new friend. Afterward, Meghan—who'd begged her mother in the school parking lot not to send her—couldn't wait to get back and inform her parents and two brothers how brave she was.

For Mark, the best moments were probably at night,

when he and Vicki zipped themselves into the little tent they shared. When he tucked her in, she looked at him with hero worship. On Friday night, she informed him he was "the greatest dad in the world." On Saturday night, she told him she'd had "the best day ever."

If other fathers could have seen the expression on her face, the school would be overrun with paternal volunteers hoping to make similarly good impressions on their own children. As a bonus, when Sunday morning rolled around, all of the girls seemed to be so tired that Mark wasn't worried about the volume in his van for the return trip. He suspected most of his passengers would fall asleep.

As the adults broke down camp, the girls took the opportunity for one last game of freeze tag in the nearby clearing. Mark kept half his attention on them and the other half on helping Shay dismantle her tent.

"It's not that I can't get it down," she said ruefully. "It pretty much fell down as soon as I touched it. I just can't figure out how to get it all to fit back in the carrier properly."

He also helped her roll up her sleeping bag, pausing when he noticed Vicki and another little girl squatting down close to the ground. He thought it would be prudent to make sure they weren't crowding something that could bite, claw or sting and was horrified for the half second that he thought he was seeing a red-and-black undulating snake. Turned out, to his vast relief, to be a throng of ladybugs crawling on a stick.

Satisfied that everyone was safe, he headed back to his packing duties. Vicki surprised him by trailing after him.

"Daddy, can the adults earn badges, too?"

"Not exactly. I'm getting pretty butterfly pins for the volunteers who help us and I have a cool leader patch coming in the mail, but the badges are mainly for you girls."

"I thought Shay was working on her healthy habits badge like we are and that you were helping her."

"Oh?" Actually, for all that Shay was a first-time camper, she'd required very little assistance and he thought she'd enjoyed herself.

Vicki nodded earnestly. "Ms. Julie and Ms. Kris said something about...the two of you playing doctor!" she declared, looking pleased to have remembered the wording.

Mark halted midstride. They said *what?* No doubt the two women hadn't meant to be overheard, but he didn't care. "Would you excuse me, Bug? I have to get finished so we can get all these girls back home before dinner, especially this little girl." He tapped her on the nose with his index finger. "Why don't you go play with your friends?"

"'Kay." She skipped back to join the game of tag.

Trying to keep his temper under control—though he couldn't remember anything in the CG handbook expressly forbidding the flaying of volunteers, it was probably frowned upon—he stalked toward Julie and Kris. They were loading up a cooler to go in the back of Julie's van.

"Oh, good." Julie straightened when she saw him. "We might need your help with... Everything okay? Did my daughter say something ugly to someone?" She sighed. "I'll have a word with her."

"Maybe you should worry about what you say," he

snapped. "And the example you two set when you deride others."

Kris drew back, shocked. "I beg your pardon."

"'Playing doctor?'" he flung at them. "Honestly, I would have expected better of you two."

Julie had the grace to flush deep crimson. "Oh, God, one of the girls overheard that? We were just, you know, being silly."

A month of frustration welled up in him. He resented that Shay had spent the early weeks of their relationship feeling like she couldn't be with him because of that kind of "silliness." He resented like hell that he could buy her dinner but felt like he wasn't supposed to reach across the table and take her hand if any of the Woodside PTA members happened to be in the establishment. Shay took it to an extreme, was ridiculously circumspect in her behavior, but it was because of thoughtless gossip like this.

"Do you know the phone calls I would have received if some little girl went home after this weekend and remarked to a parent that their troop leader was playing doctor with someone?" He kept his voice low enough not to draw the notice of the kids in the clearing, but even without yelling, his anger was palpable. "And don't think we didn't hear your comment about bringing along a date on Friday. *Lay off.*"

He'd probably made his point, but he was on a roll and couldn't stop himself. *Someone needs to say it.* Maybe these two would carry the message back to the other small-minded few who made him embarrassed to call himself a citizen of Braeden.

"Shay Morgan is a hell of a woman—she stepped in at the last minute to make sure these girls didn't lose their first trip that they'd been so excited about—and she's a hell of a principal. Do you realize that our music department was just awarded a thousand dollars because of her? My sister-in-law says she's the first principal ever to donate her time to nominating committee because she genuinely wants to help and wants to forge a good relationship with the PTA. She—"

"Mark." From behind him, Shay spoke ever so softly. "I think they get it."

He glanced at her, wondering how long she'd been there and if he'd embarrassed her with his ranting to Julie and Kris, who were both nodding frantically.

"We do. We get it," Kris promised. She looked past his shoulder. "We both like you a lot, Principal Morgan. We think you're doing a real good job. We were just… You know how girlfriends joke around, right? It can get a little risqué sometimes."

Shay's laugh was dry. "Geneva Daniels would agree with you. Water under the bridge as far as I'm concerned. Can I give you a hand with that cooler?"

Mark told himself that he was giving the three women a chance to bond by fading into the background—not slinking away out of cowardice because he didn't know whether Shay would wring his neck. After all, Kris and Julie weren't just CG volunteers, they were parents that Shay might have to work with for years to come and he perhaps hadn't been as tactful as he should have.

So when Shay came up to him a few minutes later to get the keys to the van, he asked without preamble, "Mad at me?"

"Mad?" Her eyes rounded with surprise. "Are you kidding? You made me sound magnificent. You…you not only defended me, you mentioned some of the stuff that I like the most about what I do, the things I'm most proud of. Mark, I—"

"Yeah?" He placed the keys in her palm, surreptitiously holding her hand after he should have let go.

"I love you," she said simply. "How could I not?"

A kind of delirious awe filled him. Could a man really get this lucky twice in one lifetime? "I love you, too. I—" He was cut off by a ringing sound and realized it came from the cell phone in his pocket. He had no intention of answering that when he was in the middle of one of the most important exchanges of his life.

"Shouldn't you at least check?" Shay asked ruefully. She gestured toward the girls giggling in the field. "It might be one of their parents. It could be important."

Damn, she was right. "Rain check on this conversation?" he asked as the phone continued to ring.

"How about I come over tonight after you tuck Vicki in?" Shay offered.

"She'll be in bed by seven," he said recklessly, flipping his cell phone open. *"Hello?"* It was hard to keep the exasperation out of his voice.

"Boss, I have been trying to reach you. Didn't you get my messages?"

"Roddy?" Mark frowned. "I guess not. But this isn't prime reception area and I've been surrounded by first- and second-grade girls who, as it turns out, aren't exactly the quietest creatures on God's green earth. Maybe I just didn't hear the notification beep. Is there a problem at the store?"

"Yes, and no. Bennett Coleridge is here, and he wants to see you. Immediately."

AFTER STOPPING AT WOODSIDE to deliver the girls to their parents and Shay to her car, Mark had phoned Mrs.

Norris. She'd agreed to come have dinner with Vicki so that he could talk to Coleridge. Mark had offered to meet his employer at the store, but Bennett had insisted on buying him dinner. They'd settled on the Braeden Burger Shop at five-thirty.

Mark had hoped to arrive first, to have a few minutes to compose himself and figure out what to say. He hadn't been expecting Bennett to return to North Carolina for another three or four weeks, and he'd certainly anticipated some advanced warning. Was this a surprise inspection? Had Bennett come to town so that he could form his own opinions without looking at data Mark had gathered? Had Mark hurt his credibility by being away and semi-out-of-touch all weekend?

Unfortunately, Bennett was already seated and waiting in a booth, studying the menu. *Déjà vu all over again.* This was so reminiscent of their breakfast meeting. Had it only been three months ago? It felt like a scene from an alternate dimension, from another man's life.

And yet…paradoxically, it also felt like the mere blink of an eye. He couldn't believe three months had already passed, that his chance to prove himself was almost over.

"Ah, Hathaway, there you are!" Bennett had spotted him. "Come sit down."

"Mr. Coleridge." Mark shook his hand across the table before sliding onto the bench opposite him. "I apologize if you've been waiting on me. I wasn't expecting you this weekend and I had an obligation to my daughter's troop to—"

"No need to apologize," Bennett interrupted. "I like a man who's got a well-balanced life and is loyal—he makes a better employee. If you told your daughter you were going to take her troop camping, then that's where you should have been. I apologize for inconveniencing you. It's only that I leave tomorrow and was determined to see you first."

"Are you still coming back next month?" Mark asked carefully. "Maybe we'll have more time to talk then."

Bennett's dark eyes were sad, reminding Mark of a basset hound. "Well, my wife and I will still be coming for her reunion—can't seem to get out of that—but by then, what I need to say to you will be moot, son."

No. No, no, no. Was Bennett really planning to lower the boom, shut down the store before the agreed-upon evaluation period was even over? They'd been doing better! They *would* do better. Only earlier this afternoon Mark had decided that he must be the luckiest bastard in the universe to have his amazing life and a woman like— He couldn't even think her name right now. It hurt too much.

"I don't understand, sir."

"I think you do," Bennett said levelly. "I've had an offer to buy the building. It's a solid offer but only good for a limited time. Since I was going to close the store anyway—"

"Sales are up," Mark interrupted, wishing he didn't sound so desperate. *You are yanking my life out from under me.* "Comparatively, anyway." *And what about Roddy?* He'd been working there almost as long as Mark.

"Fact of the matter is, I'm as impressed as all hell over what you've managed to accomplish in a short period of time. It would've taken a miracle to keep the place afloat and miracles are in short supply in this economy. But what you *have* done is proven yourself to me, above and beyond. Which is why I'm promoting you and transferring you to Colorado." Bennett kept talking while the waitress approached to take their drink orders, outlining some of the details.

But all Mark could hear was a shattering sound as the shards of his happiness crashed down around him.

Chapter Fourteen

It wasn't a warm night, per se, but Shay thought she could detect the underlying promise of spring as she climbed out of her car. Maybe Mark felt the same way, because he was seated outside on a padded porch bench. Or maybe he was just so eager to see her he hadn't wanted to wait inside, she thought with an inward grin. It wasn't so much arrogance as projection—she was always eager to see him.

When they'd left the campsite this afternoon, he'd seemed tense after his phone call with Roddy but all he'd tell her was, "Work stuff." Of course, shuttling four girls back to town wasn't conducive to serious conversation. Then he'd dropped her off at Woodside with a promise to text her after Vicki fell asleep. So here she was.

But Mark had yet to say hello or come toward her. He sat on the bench, his shoulders slumped as if in defeat. Was he simply worn out from the camping trip? Her heart skittered, missing a beat. What had happened to the ebullient man who'd declared his love for her earlier today?

Don't worry until you have a reason to.

"Hey," she said, suddenly feeling uncertain.

He looked up at her and even in the darkness of the

porch the bleakness in his expression was impossible to miss.

"Mark, what is it?" She sank down next to him, her hands on his arm. "What happened?"

"Coleridge is closing the store," he said bitterly. "He's selling the building and wants us to get the place ready for a going-out-of-business sale. He's offering me a month's severance pay and Roddy close to that. God." He shoved a hand through his hair. "I haven't told Roddy yet. I need to do it in person, so I decided to wait until tomorrow. I know he won't be completely surprised, but…"

She shouldn't be completely surprised, either. The very first time she'd met Mark he'd been sagging under the weight of this possibility. He'd warned her—this was ultimately one of the reasons she'd decided to be with him, because who knew how much time they'd been given?

So with all of this prior knowledge, why did she feel like she'd just been obliterated by an unexpected asteroid that fell out of the clear blue sky and turned her into a smoking crater?

She swallowed hard. "Mark, I'm so sorry. What are… what are you going to do?"

"According to Coleridge, move to Colorado. He wants to *promote* me, can you believe it?" Mark's laugh was hollow. "He said over dinner that even though the Colorado stores are doing far better, there's also more direct competition up there. He says I've shown a lot of initiative here and he'd like to see how I can apply it in other situations."

"You have done a good job," she said loyally. "I've

been proud of you. Not many people can balance work and family and a social life so well." She seemed to be stuck on autopilot. The things coming out of her mouth were little more than platitudes, the kind of "there, there" or "where life closes a door…" comments she'd make to any parent in her office facing a major upheaval.

She was in shock. After fighting it for weeks, she'd finally accepted the idea that Mark Hathaway and his adorable daughter were part of her life, a major part. And now she was losing them?

"Wh-when are you going to tell Vicki?"

"I suppose the sooner the better," he said woodenly. "Give her time to adjust to the idea. And she's going to notice that the store has Going Out Of Business plastered all over it and that Dee's crying all the time."

And that the principal of her school looks like she's just lost her best friend.

"Shay?" He sat forward. "Shay, are you crying?"

She sniffed, rubbing her eyes with the back of her hand. "I guess I am."

"Oh, honey." He pulled her into a tight hug that expressed all the painful frustration they were both feeling. Against her hair he murmured, "I do love you."

She bit her lip, unable to say it back without crying harder.

He straightened suddenly. "Marry me!"

"What?" Shay hiccuped. "That's not funny."

"I'm not kidding. I love you—you love me. Vicki—who is about to be ripped away from everything she knows—adores you. Give her the mom she so desperately wants and make me the happiest man alive. Come with us to Colorado."

"I can't do that." Shay couldn't believe what she was hearing.

"Sure you can." He sounded manic now, so caught up in his make-believe scenario that he wasn't even listening to her.

"Mark." She stood, putting distance between them. "When we left the campsite today, were you planning to propose?"

"Not consciously. But life's unpredictable. I'm rolling with it, making the best of the situation."

An outraged gasp escaped her. "*Making the best of the situation?* I was fine with you comparing our physical relationship to getting in a pool, of all things, but that is the least romantic proposal I… It's beyond unromantic. It's insulting. The part where you mentioned Vicki being ripped away from Braeden and the people here? I'm not a consolation prize, Mark. I have a life here, too. And a career I've worked hard to build. I'm not a stuffed animal you can throw in the car to cheer her up."

On some level, Shay knew that most of the fury building in her was not directed at him. It was triggered by the untenable circumstances. However, she was genuinely aghast that he thought she should alter the entire course of her future because he'd had a bad day and didn't know how to break the news to Vicki.

"Don't you want to be with me?" he asked.

"Here in Braeden, yes! But I've only known you a couple of months. I'm not about to drop everything to accept a knee-jerk proposal you're going to regret in the morning."

He jabbed a finger at her. "I'm not the one who's constantly had doubts about us and doesn't want anyone to know."

That stung. Maybe she'd questioned the wisdom of dating him at first, but that wasn't "constant" doubts. They'd been very happy for the past month—or, at least, she had. It sounded as if he was bitter about a few things.

"Look, you've just been handed a huge amount of stress that you're going to have to deal with," she said, trying to be empathetic. "Dinner at my parents is the day after tomorrow. Why don't I plan to go to that alone?" Watching her mother fawn over Mark and try to push them down the aisle would be even more painful knowing that Mark and Vicki were about to go.

"There you go again, distancing yourself!"

"Well, hell, Mark, I'm not the one moving to Colorado! I think that's going to put plenty of distance between us no matter what I say or do." *Calm down.* She was trained in dealing with conflict, defusing emotional situations. Why was she yelling at the man on his porch? "Do you remember when you told me I did the right thing by not marrying Bryan, because he obviously didn't understand my feelings or support my career? I could say the same things about you right now."

"Shay…"

Tears were welling fast and furious. "Maybe the move to Colorado will be good for you and Vicki, a fresh start. I'll…I'll call you later in the week." And with that, she hurried down the stairs to the sanctuary of her car. With any luck, she could park unseen at the end of his street and have her imminent meltdown.

WITH PRICES SLASHED, IT TOOK depressingly little time to clear out the store. Now that warm weather had returned, people were more excited about the idea of hiking, boating and playing outdoor sports. Up A Creek had been at this location for years; it didn't seem right that it could be emptied in a matter of weeks.

"We had a good run, boss," Roddy said from behind the counter. He, Cade and Mark had been taking down fixtures and cleaning up debris. "I always enjoyed working for you."

"With me," Mark said. "You as much managed this place as I did. And in case I never thanked you for stepping in after Jess died—"

Roddy waved his hand, looking emotional and embarrassed. "I'm gonna go in the back, see if we have any more coffee."

"What we really need," Cade remarked as the other man disappeared through the doorway, "is beer. How are you doing?"

I failed to keep the store open and I miss Shay with every fiber of my being. After their fight on the porch, they'd devolved by unspoken consent into a distant relationship. He called her Principal Morgan when he saw her—which didn't happen often. "Been better."

"And Vic?" Cade asked, glancing away. "How's she?"

"She's angry, scared. I went online and showed her that there's a chapter of the Campside Girls where we're moving and that she can join. I think Kris and Julie are going to take over as coleaders here when we go." Mark had told Bennett emphatically that he would not uproot Vicki before the end of her school year, the third week in May.

Dee had said Vicki could stay with them as much as necessary in order for Mark to visit Colorado, do some initial house-hunting and narrow down the choices before he took Vicki. In all of this, he'd been surprised that it wasn't more difficult to put their house on the market. It was the house he'd shared with Jess, the only house Vicki had ever lived in. But signing the documents with the real-estate agent had been more of an annoyance than a tragedy.

At the end of the day, that house was a building, and he wasn't going to miss bricks and tile. He was going to miss people. *Shay.* But if she found it that easy to walk away from him, from what they could have shared together, perhaps this was for the best.

IF SHE KEPT UP THIS KIND of behavior, Shay thought, the people who lived at the end of the street were going to report her as a possible prowler. Or a Peeping Tom, at the very least. *What are you doing, Shay?*

She'd driven all the way over here, wanting to talk to Mark, but the closer she'd gotten to his house, the more she'd panicked. What was she going to say? She wanted to apologize for their last real conversation, that fight they'd had. It ate at her, as did her mother's assertion that jobs were not as important as people.

But even though Shay thought she'd handled the entire thing gracelessly, she still believed that his "proposal" had been rash and for the wrong reasons. No doubt he'd come to that conclusion by now, too. They'd been apart nearly as long as they'd been together. If he'd gotten past it, why rock the boat by showing up on his doorstep?

Because it's the right thing to do. Even though she had no intention of going with him to Colorado—an invitation that had no doubt been rescinded anyway— she should tell him she loved him. That he'd been good to her and that she was sorry if she'd made it seem like their feelings were something shameful that should be hidden away. *If I had that to do over...*

She swallowed a lump in her throat. You didn't get to do the past over. But she had a chance now, with her present.

Starting her car up, she quickly accelerated toward his house before she could lose her nerve. But when she pulled up in front of it, she didn't see Mark's car. Instead a pretty brunette in a suit was talking to a family of four on the front porch.

The For Sale sign in the front yard featured a picture of the same brunette.

"Well, hello," the woman called out.

It was a pretty day and Shay had rolled down her windows. "Hi. I don't mean to interrupt, but...I was looking for the current owner of this house. Mr. Hathaway?"

The real-estate agent shook her head. "Sorry, honey. He's in Colorado."

"Thanks anyway." Stomach churning, Shay pulled away from the house.

He's in Colorado. Soon, it would be permanent. Maybe it was better that she hadn't found him today, hadn't put them back on speaking terms. Because she didn't think she could handle the goodbye when he left.

FROM A HOTEL ROOM IN Colorado, Mark tried to console his sister-in-law.

"I'm sorry," she blubbered into the phone. "I know I should be setting a more positive example for Vicki, but..." Her words grew muffled as she turned her head away and blew her nose. "You want to hear some good news?"

"Yes, please."

"Stacey thinks she's about to get an offer on the house. Call her when you get back into town."

That was still a couple of days away. And he missed his daughter like crazy.

"It will be hard for me to go by that subdivision," Dee admitted. "I know it's normal for families to move apart and people do it all the time without having nervous breakdowns, but…Vicki's a miniature copy of my sister. Losing her, watching the house go to another family—it feels a bit like losing Jess all over again."

"Good Lord, woman." This was Frank's voice, in the background. *"Are you trying to make him feel worse than he already does?"*

"I should go," Dee said, chagrined. "When you call tomorrow, I'll do better."

That's what she'd said yesterday.

After he hung up the phone, Mark flipped on the television, but he didn't hear any of the sportscasters on ESPN. Instead, he heard Dee's words in his head.

Like losing Jess.

When his wife had been sick, there had been nothing he could do for her, nothing he could do to fight it or to stop the inevitable. At the time, he'd felt as though he would have done anything to keep her with him. Only he hadn't been given that opportunity.

Although the past few weeks had been pretty grim, he could still recall with perfect clarity that sweet, sharp flare of joy he'd experienced when Shay told him she loved him.

He'd had no choice but to let go of Jess. But with Shay, it was different! He could fight for her. Maybe it wouldn't work out, but why wasn't he at least trying?

The entire time he'd been in Colorado, he'd been torn

between apathy and flat-out loathing for his surroundings. Objectively speaking, Colorado was a great place. But the two most important people in Mark's world were in Braeden.

Which meant he needed to be there, too.

IT WAS THE LAST MONDAY of school, the final week. In the halls all around her, students were vibrating with excitement over the upcoming break. Meanwhile, Shay moved toward her office with all the verve of a geriatric turtle.

If it weren't for a series of administrative meetings she had to attend this summer, Shay would probably crawl into bed, pull the comforter over her and stay there until August. Ironically, the superintendent had informed her that she'd been named principal of Woodside Elementary—her official title now, not an interim honor—and it hadn't done a thing to lift her spirits.

Maybe because when you got the news, there was one person you wanted to celebrate with more than anyone. And he wasn't there.

"Good morning, Ms. Morgan!" the secretary boomed when Shay walked into the office.

Shay blinked, taken aback by Roberta's volume…and her expression. Was that an actual grin? *Weird*. Maybe the secretary had summer fever. Or maybe she was just coming down with something.

"Morning, Roberta," she returned listlessly, shuffling down the hall. Now that she'd finally done it, become principal of her own school, maybe she'd proven herself. Now that she knew she had succeeded, could succeed, would it matter so much where she did it? After all, they had public schools in Colorado.

"Shay?"

With a gasp, Shay jerked up her head. And found Mark sitting at the visitor table just inside her office.

"M-Mark?" Dear God, she'd finally snapped and was hallucinating the man.

He swallowed hard. "You look beautiful."

"I look like hell," she rebutted.

"Even so." He smiled gently and she wondered if he meant it—that with lackluster hair and red-rimmed eyes she could still be beautiful to him. He raised a bag that said Book 'Em Daniels on the side. "I come bearing gifts. I understand these are your favorites."

"Geneva knows you're here?" *And didn't warn me?* The woman better have lightning-fast reflexes next time they kickboxed together.

"I've missed you." He stood and Shay fell into his arms.

"You, too." She gulped, almost afraid to ask. "Are you here to say goodbye?"

"Not exactly." For a second, she thought she heard a smile in his voice, but that was crazy. And she was loath to give up the comforting position of her head buried in his chest to check. "I thought a lot about what you said, about me expecting you to drop everything to go to Colorado—"

"I was a little harsh."

"Not really. Why should I expect you to want to come to Colorado when *I* don't even want to go? I told Bennett he should give the promotion to Roddy if he wants it."

Her heart stopped. "You did?"

"And then I got in touch with Jeffrey Frye at Hawk Summit. He can't afford me as a full-time employee, but he has some part-time marketing work he can throw my way and he's willing to help me build a PR portfolio and recommend me to other groups—like the lodge once it reopens. Think of all the babysitting money I can save if I end up a work-at-home dad. But Jeff has this crazy idea that just because he's helping me, we should honeymoon at his resort."

"H-honeymoon?"

He pulled back, threading his fingers through her hair and meeting her eyes. "That's why I'm here. I didn't come back to say goodbye. I came to ask you a question." Then, to her absolute wonderment, he dropped to one knee, reaching inside his slacks pocket to pull out a black velvet box. "Will you marry me, Shay Morgan? Not because my daughter needs a mom or because I can't bear to face Colorado alone or for any reason other than I love you. I'd like to spend the rest of our lives showing you how much."

She sank to the floor with him, nearly toppling him with kisses.

"Is that a yes?" he asked moments later, when they were trying to catch their breath.

"Yes."

Suddenly, a laugh rumbled through him.

"What is it?" Shay asked, wanting to be in on the joke.

"Well, I was just looking around—this office. It's where we first met, and I thought… It worked."

"What worked?"

"Vicki's letter." He started chuckling again. "Turns out she found me a Valentine, after all. The only one I want for the rest of my life."

* * * * *

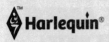

® Harlequin®

COMING NEXT MONTH

Available March 8, 2011

#1345 THE COMEBACK COWBOY
American Romance's Men of the West
Cathy McDavid

#1346 THE DOCTOR'S FOREVER FAMILY
Forever, Texas
Marie Ferrarella

#1347 SECOND CHANCE DAD
Fatherhood
Pamela Stone

#1348 THE RELUCTANT BRIDE
Anne Marie Duquette

HARCNM0211

REQUEST YOUR FREE BOOKS!

2 FREE NOVELS PLUS 2 FREE GIFTS!

Harlequin®

American Romance®

LOVE, HOME & HAPPINESS

YES! Please send me 2 FREE Harlequin American Romance® novels and my 2 FREE gifts (gifts are worth about $10). After receiving them, if I don't wish to receive any more books, I can return the shipping statement marked "cancel." If I don't cancel, I will receive 4 brand-new novels every month and be billed just $4.24 per book in the U.S. or $4.99 per book in Canada. That's a saving of at least 15% off the cover price! It's quite a bargain! Shipping and handling is just 50¢ per book in the U.S. and 75¢ per book in Canada.* I understand that accepting the 2 free books and gifts places me under no obligation to buy anything. I can always return a shipment and cancel at any time. Even if I never buy another book, the two free books and gifts are mine to keep forever.

154/354 HDN FDKS

Name	(PLEASE PRINT)
Address	Apt. #
City	State/Prov.	Zip/Postal Code
Signature (if under 18, a parent or guardian must sign)	

Mail to the **Reader Service:**
IN U.S.A.: P.O. Box 1867, Buffalo, NY 14240-1867
IN CANADA: P.O. Box 609, Fort Erie, Ontario L2A 5X3

Not valid for current subscribers to Harlequin American Romance books.

Want to try two free books from another line?
Call 1-800-873-8635 or visit www.ReaderService.com.

* Terms and prices subject to change without notice. Prices do not include applicable taxes. Sales tax applicable in N.Y. Canadian residents will be charged applicable taxes. Offer not valid in Quebec. This offer is limited to one order per household. All orders subject to credit approval. Credit or debit balances in a customer's account(s) may be offset by any other outstanding balance owed by or to the customer. Please allow 4 to 6 weeks for delivery. Offer available while quantities last.

Your Privacy—The Reader Service is committed to protecting your privacy. Our Privacy Policy is available online at www.ReaderService.com or upon request from the Reader Service.

We make a portion of our mailing list available to reputable third parties that offer products we believe may interest you. If you prefer that we not exchange your name with third parties, or if you wish to clarify or modify your communication preferences, please visit us at www.ReaderService.com/consumerschoice or write to us at Reader Service Preference Service, P.O. Box 9062, Buffalo, NY 14269. Include your complete name and address.

HARI1

JEMIMA yanked open a drawer in the sideboard to find Alfie's birth certificate. Her son was her husband's child. It was a question of telling the truth whether she liked it or not. She extended the certificate to Alejandro.

"This has to be nonsense," Alejandro asserted.

"Well, if you can find some other way of explaining how I managed to give birth by that date and Alfie not be yours, I'd like to hear it," Jemima challenged.

Alejandro glanced up, golden eyes bright as blades and as dangerous. "All this proves is that you must still have been pregnant when you walked out on our marriage. It does not automatically follow that the child is mine."

"'I know it doesn't suit you to hear this news now and I really didn't want to tell you. But I can't lie to you about it. Someday Alfie may want to look you up and get acquainted."

"If what you have just told me is the truth, if that little boy does prove to be mine, it was vindictive and extremely selfish of you to leave me in ignorance!"

Jemima paled. "When I left you, I had no idea that I was still pregnant."

"Two years is a long period of time, yet you made no attempt to inform me that I might be a father. I will want DNA tests to confirm your claim before I make any decision about what I want to do."

"Do as you like," she told him curtly. "*I* know who Alfie's father is and there has never been any doubt of his identity."

"I will make arrangements for the tests to be carried out and I will see you again when the result is available," Alejandro drawled with lashings of dark Spanish masculine reserve.

"I'll contact a solicitor and start the divorce," Jemima proffered in turn.

Alejandro's eyes narrowed in a piercing scrutiny that made her uncomfortable. "It would be foolish to do anything before we have that DNA result."

"I disagree," Jemima flashed back. "I should have applied for a divorce the minute I left you!"

Alejandro quirked an ebony brow. "And why didn't you?"

Jemima dealt him a fulminating glance but said nothing, merely moving past him to open her front door in a blunt invitation for him to leave.

"I'll be in touch," he delivered on the doorstep.

What is Alejandro's next move? Perhaps rekindling their marriage is the only solution! But will Jemima agree?

*Find out in Lynne Graham's
exciting new romance
JEMIMA'S SECRET*

*Available March 2011
from Harlequin Presents®.*

Start your Best Body today with these top 3 nutrition tips!

1. **SHOP THE PERIMETER OF THE GROCERY STORE:** The good stuff—fruits, veggies, lean proteins and dairy—always line the outer edges of the store. When you veer into the center aisles, you enter the temptation zone, where the unhealthy foods live.

2. **WATCH PORTION SIZES:** Most portion sizes in restaurants are nearly twice the size of a true serving and at home, it's easy to "clean your plate." Use these easy serving guidelines:
   - Protein: the palm of your hand
   - Grains or Fruit: a cup of your hand
   - Veggies: the palm of two open hands

3. **USE THE RAINBOW RULE FOR PRODUCE:** Your produce drawers should be filled with every color of fruits and vegetables. The greater the variety, the more vitamins and other nutrients you add to your diet.

Find these and many more helpful tips in

YOUR BEST BODY NOW
by
TOSCA RENO
WITH STACY BAKER

Bestselling Author of
THE EAT-CLEAN DIET®

Available wherever books are sold!

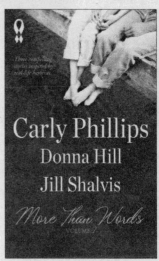